GINGERBREAD

Gingerbread
Peter Cave

MAINSTREAM
PUBLISHING

EDINBURGH AND LONDON

First published in Great Britain in 1993 by
MAINSTREAM PUBLISHING COMPANY
(EDINBURGH) LTD
7 Albany Street
Edinburgh EH1 3UG

ISBN 1 85158 556 7

A catalogue record for this book is available from the British
Library

Typeset in Garamond

Printed in Great Britain by BPCC Wheatons, Exeter

*For Holly, who never did believe
in witches*

Prologue

'A long time ago there lived an old woman, who was also an enchantress; and her daughter was the most beautiful creature under the sun. But the old woman was ever scheming how to entice men, in order to kill them . . .'

Simon Barrow let his voice drop gradually to a whisper, finally stopping altogether. He looked down at his little sister's peaceful face, her eyes gently closed and the residual traces of a dreamy smile still on her lips.

She was fast asleep at last. The customary bedtime story had achieved its desired effect. Simon closed the pages of the fairy-tale book and placed it gently on the bedside table. Reaching over the thick volume, he switched on Nicola's favourite night-light — a small earthenware cottage modelled on the gingerbread house from *Hansel and Gretel* — and stood up. He took one last fond look at his sleeping sister and backed quietly out of her bedroom, closing the door silently behind him and leaving her to her dreams.

But while Nicola dreamed, somewhere not far away, on the outskirts of the city, Betty Duncan was living another chapter of her private nightmare.

If such things as witches really existed, then Betty Duncan might well have been mistaken for one. Once undeniably beautiful, time had been particularly cruel to her. Her face was now creased and lined, with a fatty build-up above the cheekbones which had pushed puffy bags up under her eyes, giving them a sunken, almost malevolent appearance. Her black hair, once long and lustrous, now hung greasy and lank over her shoulders. At sixty, she was a hag, a crone — her mind as twisted into knotted folds of bitterness as her flesh.

Her home, too, had a surreal, almost menacing look of decay. The cottage, once lovingly built by her long-dead husband in Dunleath Woods as an escape from the city, was now little more than a crumbling, rotting shack. The surrounding grounds, originally laid out with flower-beds and a herb garden, were now festooned with weeds and the wild brambles which had grown to within a few feet of the wooden walls.

Yet inside, the cottage was cramped, but cosy — warmly carpeted and fitted out with quality furnishings and a few of life's simpler luxuries. The kitchen-cum-parlour was especially clean and bright-looking, reflecting Betty Duncan's enduring love and remaining interest in life — cooking and baking. Cakes, pies, puddings and especially gingerbread men were constantly baking in the oven of her old-fashioned open-range cooker — mostly to lie around, uneaten, until they were stale and had to be thrown away. The children who had eaten the goodies no longer filled the cottage with their laughter — but Betty continued to bake nevertheless.

But tonight, Betty Duncan had no time for baking. There was more urgent, far more grisly work to be done.

Panting with the effort, Betty dragged the naked corpse of a man down the wooden stairs by his feet. The man's head, wrapped tightly in a heavily bloodstained rag, thumped against each stair tread in turn as she pulled him laboriously from step to step. Reaching the foot of the stairs, she dragged him across the parlour carpet to the back door and, opening it, out into the darkness of the yard.

Some twenty feet from the house, a large metal incinerator was just visible in the faint light from the cottage window. Betty dragged her burden across to it and bent to grip the body under the armpits, hauling it up until she could throw one limp arm over the metal rim of the container, hooking the cadaver in position. Thus propped up, it was possible, with a little effort, to lift the body by its feet again and dump it, head first, into the incinerator. Sweating in the heat of the sultry August night, Betty set about her task, eventually managing to heave the body in on top of the pile of sticks and logs she had already stacked inside the container.

She returned to the house, coming out again a few moments later with a bundle of clothing, a briefcase and a large can of petrol.

She dumped the clothes into the bin and hefted the briefcase by its handle. In small brass embossed letters, the owner's name glinted in the reflected light from the window. Betty paused momentarily to wonder who or what Phillip Chalmers had been in life, then tossed the case into the bin and emptied the petrol can on top of it.

She struck a match and tossed it in, stepping back quickly as the incinerator erupted into flames with a dull *whoosh*. She stood for some time, as though hypnotised by the leaping, dancing flames. In the hellish glow, her aged face looked even more eerie and witch-like.

Finally, as the flames started to die down, Betty turned and walked slowly back towards the cottage, her heart and spirits heavy with the burden of it all.

It was not over yet. Perhaps the private hell she had created for herself would never be over.

9

Chapter One

The forest seemed a peaceful, almost idyllic place in the soft, muted light of an autumn morning. Even the cottage appeared to be a natural part of the order of things, its weather-beaten woodwork and irregular geometry blending in perfectly with the carpet of yellow and brown fallen leaves and the newly bare branches of the surrounding trees.

Tom Barrow leaned back against the silver bark of a birch tree, facing the cottage and apparently daydreaming while his two children played happily amongst the bushes and brambles. To the casual observer, it would have looked like the most innocent of scenes. A family day-out in the woods — a proud father relaxing in the October sunshine while his twelve-year-old son and five-year-old daughter chased each other and picked blackberries.

But the casual observer would not have known that it was not mere chance which had brought Tom Barrow to this particular spot in the forest. Or, indeed, that he had very good reason to study the cottage closely.

An excited yell from his son Simon interrupted his concentration.

'Dad, look — I've found some badger tracks.'

Barrow tore his eyes away from the cottage and pushed himself away from the inclined trunk of the tree. He strolled over to where Simon crouched near to the ground, examining some faint paw prints in the soft mud beneath a clump of bushes.

Barrow bent down beside his son, studying the prints carefully before nodding his head. 'You're right, son. Well spotted. There must be a sett nearby.'

Simon rose to his feet, smiling proudly and basking in his father's praise. 'Do you think I'll make a good detective?' he asked.

Barrow wrapped his arm around his son's shoulders, hugging him. 'Oh, I'm sure you will.' He looked over towards his daughter, who had now filled a large jug with blackberries. 'Nicola, I think we have enough now. It's time to go.'

With one last backward glance at the cottage, Barrow waited for his daughter to rejoin them and began to lead the way back to the car.

Detective Sergeant Mike Jardine was another man who had dual motives for being in a certain place at a certain time. He accompanied DC Jackie Reid as she strolled through the children's section of one of Glasgow's biggest bookshops, ostensibly as an adviser on suitable reading material for her young nephew. But his eyes were elsewhere, his mind years away in the past.

'How about this one for an eight-year-old?' Jackie was asking, holding up a book of bedtime stories.

Jardine didn't even look at the cover. 'Too young,' he commented, dismissively. 'Kids grow up far quicker these days.' He clutched the hardback book in his own hand tightly, still watching the queue of people over in the adult section of the shop.

It was a book-signing session by the author, an extremely attractive young woman in her early thirties. Jardine glanced down at the book he held in his hand, turning it over to look again at the picture of the young woman on the back cover. Very attractive indeed.

The queue appeared to be thinning out. Seeing his chance, Jardine suddenly walked away from Jackie Reid and strode over, taking his place behind the two women who were waiting to have their copies signed. With something of a shock, Jardine realised that his heart seemed to be fluttering erratically and he suddenly felt very young, and very foolish.

Suddenly he was at the front of the queue, gazing down on the soft, dark brown hair of the woman hunched over the signing desk. Fighting to control his voice, Jardine placed his copy down on the desk.

'Could you sign this one, please?'

Gemma Normanton picked up the volume automatically, opening it at the flyleaf with her pen poised. She had been signing copies for over three hours now, and it was starting to become a rather dull routine. But it was her first book, she was glad her publishers had decided on a big publicity launch, and it seemed only right to play her part. She switched on the fixed smile, started the little rehearsed speech and looked up.

'Would you like it dedicated to anyone in partic —'

The shock of recognition cut her voice in mid-speech. The routine smile turned into a genuine beam of pleasure. Gemma jumped to her feet, leaning forward impulsively and kissing him on the cheek.

'Michael! Michael Jardine. How wonderful to see you. What are you doing these days?'

Jardine shuffled his feet awkwardly, still feeling rather sheepish. 'I read that you were doing this signing, so I thought I'd come along,' he muttered. Out of the corner of his eye he noticed Jackie Reid hovering in the background, not sure whether she might be interrupting something or not. Jardine took advantage of her presence to make conversation.

'Oh, this is Jackie. She's a colleague. I joined the police force, you see.'

Jackie stepped forward, accepting her invitation into the conversation. 'Well, don't sound as though you're apologising for it,' she put in jokingly.

Gemma was shaking her head slowly, as though she could not quite believe what she was hearing. She looked at Jardine again. 'You, join the police force? I think I heard a rumour, but I just didn't believe it. You were going to become an airline pilot.'

Jardine was relaxing now. References to their shared past made him feel more comfortable. He smiled wistfully. 'I wanted to be a lot of things when I was seventeen,' he said.

Jackie could not help putting in her own slightly sarcastic comment. 'Just think what the aviation industry lost.'

Jardine ignored her. 'Look, what are you doing for lunch?' he asked Gemma.

She looked apologetic. 'Sorry, but there's a wine and cheese publicity do in the offices upstairs. First book launch — you know the sort of thing. Meet the press, chat to people, the usual routine.'

Jardine's face registered his disappointment. Gemma paused, thinking for a moment, then her face brightened. 'Look, why don't you both come up as my guests? I don't see why I can't have a few of my oldest and dearest friends around me.'

Jackie and Jardine exchanged a brief glance, which Gemma took to be acceptance. 'Great. That's settled, then. You two go ahead and grab yourselves a glass of wine and a nibble, and I'll be up in about five minutes.'

She pointed to the stairway which led to the upstairs offices as another man stepped up with a copy of her book in his hand, waiting for a signature. Gemma flashed Jardine one last fond smile and got back to the business in hand.

'Would you like it dedicated to anyone in particular?'

'Oldest and dearest, eh?' Jackie murmured as they headed for the stairs. 'Well, are you going to tell me the story?'

Jardine had a faraway smile on his face. 'She was the best-looking girl in my school,' he murmured. 'She always wanted to be a writer, I remember.'

'I had a crush on the best-looking boy in my school,' Jackie put in. 'He was going to be a transplant surgeon, as I recall. You should see him now. Seventeen stone with a beer gut and a chippie in Anniesland.'

But Jardine wasn't really interested in Jackie's schoolday crushes. What he had shared with Gemma Normanton back in those heady days of youth and boundless optimism had been something a lot deeper, a lot more serious.

'We nearly got engaged,' he said wistfully.

Jackie looked up at him in surprise. Somehow a love-struck, impulsive Mike Jardine didn't quite fit in with the modern image. 'You were going to get engaged — when you were at *school*?'

Jardine laughed. 'No, when we were seventeen,' he corrected, remembering the difference.

They had reached the top of the stairs. The press reception was laid out along the open corridor outside the offices, with tables of wine and snacks and a large display of Gemma's book and publicity photographs. A slightly frenetic PR-type woman practically pounced on them as they rounded the top of the stairway, beaming a welcome.

'Hello! Super that you could manage to come. What magazine are you from, by the way?'

Jardine gave her a slightly apologetic smile. 'Actually, we're just personal friends of Miss Normanton,' he told her.

'Oh.' The woman's welcoming smile faded abruptly. She cast her eyes nervously about, seeking another target. 'Well, if you'll excuse me, I have to go and talk to the literary critic of the *Morning Post*.' She disappeared as quickly as she had come, switching on the beaming smile again as she plunged into the little knot of people clustered around the buffet table.

'It's another world,' Jackie observed, glancing around at the smartly suited literary types, journalists and well-heeled publishers. She gazed up at Jardine and the look in her eyes carried an implicit warning. Not the world of a Glasgow copper.

Jardine failed to see any significance in the remark. He was still feeling the soft touch of Gemma's lips on his cheek, and remembering the genuine warmth with which she had recognised and greeted him. The intervening years and the different paths their lives had taken were forgotten, as though they had never existed.

He crossed to the nearest open space at the drinks table and helped himself to two glasses of mineral water. He carried them back and handed one to Jackie, edging her into a quiet and neutral corner. They sipped at their drinks for a couple of minutes, totally ignored by everyone else in the room.

'I do hope you're not feeling left out,' came a friendly female voice in Jardine's ear. He turned, gratefully recognising Gemma's voice.

'No, we're fine — really.'

Gemma looked at the glass in his hand with some surprise. 'What's that you're drinking?'

'Mineral water,' Jardine said innocently, unprepared for the amusement it would cause her.

Gemma finally managed to control her laughter. 'This is the Mike Jardine who used to bring half a bottle of vodka to school and keep it in his desk?'

Jardine looked highly embarrassed, aware that Jackie Reid was regarding him curiously. 'Don't let everybody know.' he protested awkwardly.

His embarrassment spread to Jackie, who realised that besides being the 'everybody' in question, she was also in danger of becoming the proverbial spare bride at the wedding. It was time to make an exit, she decided, though not necessarily a discreet one.

'Well, I guess I have enough to fill the front page,' she announced suddenly to Jardine. 'I'll see you back in the office.' She turned to Gemma, smiling sweetly. 'Thanks for the invite.'

Gemma watched her as she pushed her way through the

little throng of journalists then looked up at Jardine, a question in her eyes. 'Just a colleague?'

Jardine gave an emphatic nod. 'Just.' He found it rather flattering that Gemma looked relieved. 'And congratulations on the book by the way,' he added.

'Which reminds me — I never did get around to signing it for you.' Gemma took the book from Jardine's hand and opened it, writing inside the flyleaf. She closed the book again and handed it back. 'Now, Mike, I really am sorry but I have to go and talk to some people.'

She kissed him on the cheek again and walked away. Jardine watched her go with regret, finally looking down at the book and opening it to see what she had written.

There were just two short words, followed by a question mark. 'Dinner tonight?'

Jardine felt like a little boy with a brand new bike all the way back to Maryhill Police Station.

Jim Taggart was not in the best of moods. Perversely, it was not because he was under pressure, but the very opposite. Things had been ominously quiet for nearly three weeks, and Taggart distrusted quiet periods. They had a nasty habit of turning out to be the lull before the storm, and he found the waiting period intensely frustrating. His sense of stagnation was not improved by the sight of Jardine relaxing at his desk with a book in his hand as he marched into the office.

'What's this — a public library?' he enquired sarcastically.

Jardine sat up with a start, dropping Gemma's book on to his desk. 'Sorry, sir.'

Taggart strode over and picked the book up, reading the title. '*Flickering Candles*?'

'It's about the condemned prisoners on America's Death Row,' Jardine explained. 'How they cope with their lives while they're waiting for death.'

Taggart grunted, unimpressed. 'I thought you'd got over that woolly liberal stage.'

16

'It's written by an old schoolfriend of mine,' Jardine added with unmistakable pride in his voice.

Taggart glanced at Gemma's photograph on the back cover, raising one eyebrow sardonically. 'Not so old,' he observed. It was almost a compliment. He opened the book, noticing the handwritten invitation inside. Feeling slightly embarrassed, as though he had invaded Jardine's privacy in some way, he handed the book back. 'Just keep your mind on the job,' he muttered, turning away to go to his own office.

Jardine glanced sideways at Jackie Reid, a grin on his face. 'I think he'd like me to stay in after school,' he whispered.

He had forgotten his superior's uncannily keen sense of hearing. Taggart stopped in his tracks outside his office, whirling round.

'Aye — and you can take a hundred lines as well,' he barked, before storming through the door and slamming it behind him.

Chapter Two

Agnetha, the family au pair in the Barrow household, had done a wonderful job with the collected blackberries, turning them into a delicious fruit pie which was now gracing the supper table.

As chief collector, Nicola had begged for the privilege of cutting the pie and was now fulfilling that important function, her small hands holding the sharp knife being guided by those of her adoring and protective father.

Simon accepted his slice of pie and began to tuck in with relish. He looked up at his father over the top of his plate. 'Are you working tonight?' he asked.

Barrow nodded apologetically. 'I'm afraid so. And I'll probably be late home.'

'How late?' Simon wanted to know.

Barrow smiled indulgently at his son, knowing the reason behind the questions. '*Very* late,' he said. 'And no, you can't come with me. Not on this particular case.'

Simon managed to mask his disappointment. 'What case

are you working on?'

'Missing person,' Barrow said. He tapped his cardboard folder on the table beside him. 'I have to find out why a woman's husband just disappeared one night.'

Simon was already fascinated. His enthusiasm for his father's work took the form of near hero-worship, choosing to see his dad as a sort of amalgam of every TV sleuth and fictional superhero all rolled into one.

'Why do you think he went missing?' he asked.

Barrow shrugged. 'Who knows, Simon. It just happens sometimes. Adults just decide to disappear for one reason or another.'

'But why just you?' Simon went on. 'If children go missing, the whole police force is out looking for them.'

It was a good question, and one that Barrow didn't really have a convincing answer for. 'Well, I suppose you might say that grown-ups have a right to disappear if they want to,' he explained finally. 'And children don't.'

It seemed to suffice. 'Oh,' Simon murmured. He lapsed into silence, finishing his piece of pie and scraping the last crumbs and traces of juice from his plate. His hunger was satisfied, but not his curiosity. Reaching out he turned the file around so that he could read the name printed on the cover. CHALMERS, Phillip.

Simon had one last question. 'Who is Phillip Chalmers?'

Barrow picked up the file, standing up from the table and preparing to leave. 'He's just a man,' he said. 'Just a man who went missing one night about two months ago.'

Fully dressed up for a dinner date, Gemma Normanton was not merely a highly attractive woman, she was stunning. Jardine regarded her adoringly over the restaurant table, his face glowing with pride. He was sure that he was the envy of every other man in the place.

'So, what made you specialise in crime writing?' he asked conversationally.

Gemma picked at her sole bonne femme daintily. 'I worked as court correspondent for the Manchester *Evening Times* for a few years, until they eventually promoted me to the crime desk. Then I met this American guy, went to New York and got a job as a crime reporter on the *Daily News*. Believe me, you really do see crime over there.'

'I can believe that,' Jardine agreed heartily. He ate another mouthful of food before speaking again. 'I read part of your book this afternoon.'

Gemma leaned forward over the table. 'What did you think?'

'You seem to think that a lot of them are innocent,' Jardine said. 'Do you really believe that?'

Gemma laid down her fork gently on the table. She looked across at Jardine, her beautiful face suddenly very serious. 'You'd have to visit Death Row to understand,' she said, not sounding at all patronising. 'It's just . . . well, it's just an experience that changes your whole perspective on life. All those human lives just waiting to be extinguished. Like flickering candles.'

'Ah, so that's where you got the title,' Jardine murmured. 'I did wonder.' He paused, glancing away slightly so that he was not looking directly into her eyes. 'And the American guy? What happened to him?'

'He had a wife and five children in Seattle,' Gemma answered frankly. She shrugged, as if dismissing the entire episode in her life. 'Still, I did get to travel, see some of the world. And now I'm back in dear old Glasgow — living with my mum and dad, would you believe?'

'And launched on a promising new career,' Jardine put in. For a moment Gemma had sounded as if the present was just a penance, a temporary punishment for past sins. He raised his glass of tonic water. 'Let's drink a toast to the future of Gemma Normanton, novelist.'

Gemma smiled. 'But you're not, not really,' she pointed out. 'How can you be a policeman and not drink? It seems almost a contradiction in terms.'

Jardine sipped at his tonic water. 'I get my kicks in other ways,' he said with a slight wink.

'So, how come you never got married?' Gemma wanted to know. 'I seem to remember that you were always keen on the idea of being a family man.'

Jardine shrugged philosophically. 'Just never met the right person, I suppose.' He looked at her with a thoughtful expression in his eyes. 'I wonder how we might have worked out together?'

Gemma's reaction was instant, and totally dismissive. 'I shudder to think,' she said, with a faint grimace. 'We were far too young. We'd have held each other back. I mean, can you imagine me with a string of babies? I've met too many people who jumped into marriage and regretted it.'

Jardine was quite taken aback by the sheer passion of Gemma's little speech, and it showed on his face.

'Sorry, I didn't mean it to sound like a diatribe,' Gemma said after a brief pause.

Jardine forced a smile. 'Keep it up. I might find out where I went wrong.'

Gemma reached across the table for his hand, holding it for a lingering moment. 'No one went wrong, Mike. We just grew up,' she said gently.

Tom Barrow sat in his parked car with the engine and lights switched off, the Chalmers file open on the passenger seat beside him. He stared morosely out through the windscreen, feeling tired, irritable and more than a little nervous. He didn't like this part of the city. Unpleasant, violent things happened here — especially at night. He glanced at his watch, disappointed to see that it was still only 10.30. It was shaping up to be a long, weary night, Barrow realised, sighing to himself. These late-night stake-outs were one of the most depressing aspects of the job, but unfortunately all too frequent and necessary.

More from boredom than anything else, he picked up the

file from the seat beside him and began to sift through its contents for perhaps the fourth time that evening. He selected a small white piece of card and stared at it in the dim light from the nearest street-lamp, reading the crudely printed message yet again. Probably printed on one of those do-it-yourself machines found in shopping malls and supermarkets, Barrow decided. Discreet, anonymous and with no one to check back to.

Yet the simple piece of card represented his biggest clue so far to the mystery of Phillip Chalmers' disappearance. And if it meant what Barrow suspected it did, then he had stumbled on to something far bigger, and far nastier, than he could have imagined.

He slipped the card back into the folder and stared out through the windscreen again. To cheer himself up, he thought of his beloved home and family, knowing that it was the one thing which always seemed to help him through the most unpleasant situations.

Simon Barrow lay on his bed listening to a tape of favourite classical overtures on his cassette recorder and looking at his leather-bound volume of *Grimm's Fairy Tales*. Not really reading, he flipped the pages idly, eventually turning to the one lavish colour-plate picture which had started to fascinate him so strangely over the past few months.

The picture was of a beautiful young princess dressed in a flowing blue cloak and hood, with her lovely, long blonde hair cascading to her waist. As ever, Simon's eyes travelled to the bodice of the white dress which the princess wore beneath the cloak, noticing the faintest suggestion of cleavage, a soft, swelling roundness of creamy flesh.

Although he didn't understand it yet, Simon had started to feel the first instinctive stirrings of adolescence. Inside the child, the man had awoken and was beginning to assert himself.

The bedroom door opened suddenly. Simon started, snapping the book shut and feeling slightly guilty for some vague reason he could not quite comprehend. Agnetha stood in the doorway looking rather annoyed.

'Your music is too loud,' she complained. 'Now Nicola, she is woken up and wanting a story.'

Simon reached out and adjusted the volume control on the cassette player. 'Can't you read her one?'

Agnetha pouted. 'I watch film,' she said, in her slightly stilted English. 'You wake her — you read to her.' As if the matter was now settled, she turned and walked away back to the lounge.

Simon sighed wearily, switched off the music and picked up the fairy-tale book. He flipped through it until he found the story of Hansel and Gretel and, marking the open pages with his thumb, carried the book into Nicola's bedroom.

Barrow tailed the battered Fiat Panda at a safe and discreet distance, driving with only his sidelights switched on. There was a grim smile of satisfaction on his face as the Panda turned off the main road towards Dunleath Woods. Although the implications were horrifying, it meant that his theory had been correct. Everything, eventually, led back to that cottage. There was no longer any doubt in his mind. His suspicions, bizarre as they were, stood up to the cold, harsh light of reality.

Barrow pulled his car to a halt in a lay-by as the Panda turned into the narrow lane which led up to the cottage. He switched off the engine and waited for several minutes. Finally, when he was sure that the Panda was not coming back, he climbed out of his car and began to cut through the dark and forbidding woods towards the rear of the cottage.

There was a single light in one of the upstairs windows. Cautiously, Barrow skirted around to where the Panda was parked. Touching her bonnet with his fingers to confirm the warmth of the engine, he stepped back and made a note of the licence number. Then he headed towards the large metal incinerator which he had noted on his previous visit. If his suspicions were correct, there might be some traces of ash or half-burnt debris which would yield forensic evidence.

Intent on his mission, Barrow failed to see the slight movement of the curtain in one of the unlit upstairs windows. He approached the incinerator, unaware that a keen pair of eyes were now following his every move.

Chapter Three

Barrow pulled into his driveway and fingered the automatic garage door control fitted into the car dashboard. As the doors slid soundlessly upwards, he drove into the garage, switched off the engine and climbed out, glad to be back to the comfort and security of his own home.

Closing the garage behind him, he trudged wearily to the front door and let himself in, throwing his coat carelessly over the hall rack and loosening his tie. He walked directly into the lounge and headed for the drinks cabinet. What he needed right now was a good stiff drink. Pouring himself a large measure of whisky, Barrow headed for his favourite easy chair to try and relax.

The doorbell rang, making him jump slightly. Barrow glanced at his watch, noting the lateness of the hour and muttering a curse under his breath. Still carrying the whisky glass in his hand, he went to find out who his nocturnal visitor could possibly be.

Upstairs, the sound of the doorbell had woken Simon

from a light and fitful sleep. Snapping on his bedside lamp, he threw back the duvet and swung his legs over the edge of the bed. Clad in his pyjamas, Simon crossed to the bedroom door, opened it and stepped out on to the landing, padding quietly towards the stairway.

He heard the sound of the front door being opened and a muffled cry of surprise a split second before he reached the head of the stairs and could see down into the front hallway. Simon watched, terrified, as a menacing figure in a caped mac and hood leapt forwards through the open doorway into the hall, pushing his father back against the wall. The caped figure held one hand high in the air, and Simon could see the wicked blade of an open cut-throat razor glinting in the light. Even as Simon watched, his terror mounting, the evil weapon sliced down towards his father's face and throat.

Simon screamed once — a single denial of the horror he was witnessing — as his father's blood spurted out in a vermilion fountain, spraying his attacker and the wall behind him. The caped figure whirled round in alarm at the sound, gazing up the stairs towards the boy who stood there, frozen with shock. He was standing almost immediately under the hall light, and the effect of shadow, and the shrouding of the cape hood, made him look like some sort of dark, almost faceless fiend.

The shock of adrenaline pumping into Simon's system triggered the flight or fight response. His only thought was for his own life, and that of his sister. Simon turned and began to run towards Nicola's bedroom, even as the attacker started after him and began to bound up the stairs.

Simon fell into Nicola's bedroom, slamming the door behind him and dragging a chest of drawers into place as a temporary barricade. He ran to his sister's sleeping form, shaking her urgently.

'Nicola! Wake up! We have to get away.'

The child stirred, her eyes widening in surprise at the sight of her distraught brother bending over her bed. Simon tore back the covers and snatched her by the hand, hauling her to her feet. He dragged her to the bedroom window and threw it open, releasing the emergency fire ladder and pushing her through the open window.

Behind him, there was a furious pounding on the bedroom door, and the chest of drawers began to move.

Jardine drove at a relaxed pace, a self-satisfied smile upon his face. His eyes were on the road ahead, but he wasn't really concentrating. His mind was still with Gemma, the excellence of the meal, and the way that their date had gone so well, so naturally, that it seemed they had always been together, a perfect couple.

A sudden flash of something light in the road ahead snapped his attention back to driving. In the beam of his headlights Jardine saw a young boy and a smaller girl, clad only in their nightclothes, running hand in hand down the middle of the road.

Muttering a curse, Jardine stamped on the brakes and threw the steering wheel over, slewing the car to a halt at the side of the road. He snapped open his seat belt and reached for the door handle, ready to leap out and confront the children with an angry tirade.

The look of utter terror on the young boy's face stilled his tongue. Jardine knelt down in the road, holding out his hands to stop them as they ran towards him.

'Hold it. What's the matter?'

Simon's voice was jerky and broken. 'Help us, please. Someone's killing our father.'

Jardine straightened, his eyes roving the area around him. 'Where?'

Simon pointed towards his house, back down the street. 'The house there — with the stained-glass porch. Hurry, please.'

Jardine moved swiftly, his first concern for the children's safety. He pushed them to the car, opening the rear door and bundling them inside.

'Stay there, both of you,' he snapped. 'Push down the locks and stay there until I come back.' He slammed the door and turned towards the house that Simon had indicated, breaking into a loping run.

The front door was still half-open. With the obvious panic and concern of the children overriding his normal instinct for caution, Jardine pushed it fully open and ran in, his eyes darting from side to side.

It was impossible to miss the blood on the wall and carpet. Jardine's eyes followed a gory, glistening trail which led across the hallway and up the stairs.

The blood finally triggered his sense of caution. It was fresh, so it was more than possible that the killer was still in the house. Pausing only to glance into the lounge, Jardine moved back to the staircase and began to climb slowly, taking care not to step in the blood.

Barrow's body lay sprawled across the top landing, the upstairs telephone extension in his hand. Jardine dropped to one knee, examining the man's injuries. It was not a pleasant sight. Barrow's throat was slashed several times, his head lying in a huge pool of blood. He was quite dead.

A sudden faint thumping sound made Jardine tense up, his ears straining to identify the source of the sound. It came again, from inside one of the bedrooms. Jardine rose to his feet slowly, his mind and body primed for action. He crept slowly towards the bedroom door, which was slightly ajar, and pushed on it with his fingertips. The door appeared to be jammed in some way. Stepping back, Jardine positioned his shoulder and ran forwards, throwing the whole of his body weight against the door.

There was a loud crash as the chest of drawers wedged against the inside of the door fell over. Jardine threw himself in through the gap which he had opened up and scanned the interior of the bedroom in an instant. It was empty. On the other side of the room his eyes took in the open window, with the curtains blowing in the breeze. There was a fallen table lamp dangling off a bedside table by its flex. As Jardine

28

looked, the breeze moved the lamp again, making it thump gently against the wall.

Still cautious, Jardine moved across the bedroom towards the window and peered out, noting the dropped safety ladder which ran down to the ground outside. Jardine's eyes covered the back garden, searching for any sign of movement. There was none. Finally, he pulled his head in from the open window and began to straighten up.

He only vaguely sensed movement behind him and began to turn, his heart pounding. But it was too late. Something heavy smashed across the back of his head and blackness descended. Jardine slumped to the floor, out cold.

The outside of the house was already a hive of police activity as Taggart arrived on the scene. He walked through a virtual corridor of flashing blue lights and up the driveway. Jardine sat on the front step, having his bleeding head tended to by an ambulance attendant.

'You got here fast,' Taggart said, having ascertained that his colleague was not seriously hurt.

Jardine looked up at him with a sour expression on his face. 'Thanks for the concern,' he said cynically. He waved the ambulance man away with a faint, grateful movement of his hand and struggled to stand up, wincing at the pain in his throbbing head. He propped himself up against the door jamb, gesturing across to where DC Reid was trying to comfort the distraught Agnetha.

'The au pair, sir,' Jardine explained.

Taggart glanced at the ambulance attendant, who was still hovering around Jardine. He gave the man a faint nod, jerking his head in the direction of the waiting ambulance.

Understanding, the man closed in on Jardine again, laying one arm across his shoulders. 'Come on, sir, let's get you to hospital for a check-up.'

Jardine allowed himself to be propelled towards the ambulance, as Taggart strode across to Jackie Reid and Agnetha. The au pair was in a state of mild hysteria, but still just about capable of talking rationally, Taggart decided.

'What happened?'

Agnetha looked towards him, but her eyes were darting about distractedly.

'I hear a crash and wake up,' she said, her voice shaky. 'Outside I see Mr Barrow, dead, and then I see this man in Nicola's bedroom and I think perhaps he is the murderer, so I hit him with vase. I not know he is detective.'

Jackie Reid patted her on the shoulder comfortingly. 'It's all right. He's fine, you haven't hurt him. You did a brave thing.'

The reassurance seemed to help, Agnetha looked calmer for a while, until a new wave of fear seemed to strike her. 'The children. I must look after them. Where are they?' she blurted out.

Jackie Reid gestured to a uniformed officer who came over carrying a blanket and wrapped it around the au pair's shoulders.

'The children are safe — with a neighbour,' Jackie told her. 'Now you just try to calm down, go with this officer and I'll talk to you later. All right?'

Agnetha nodded absently and let herself be led away towards one of the waiting police cars.

Jackie turned to Taggart. 'Mike is okay, isn't he?'

Taggart nodded. 'He'll probably have a headache for a few hours. What was he doing, anyway? Playing the Seventh Cavalry?'

Jackie frowned at him. 'He thought he might be preventing a murder being committed,' she said in Jardine's defence. She gestured into the house. 'Do you want to see inside?'

Without waiting for an answer, she led the way through the open front door, pausing just inside the hallway and pointing down at the first patch of blood on the carpet.

'This is obviously where the attack happened, sir. The victim made it as far as the top of the stairs — probably to see his kids.' She turned towards the stairs. 'Oh, watch out for the blood, sir.'

Taggart's eyes took in the gore soaked into the carpet and smeared liberally over the wall and banister. 'I could hardly miss it,' he grunted sarcastically. He followed Jackie Reid upstairs towards Barrow's body.

Dr Andrews, the pathologist, was already on the job. He looked up at Taggart as he approached, his face grim. 'Apparently he had the telephone in his hand when the au pair found him. She used it to call the police, then put it back in the cradle.'

Taggart looked down at the corpse with all the professional detachment he could muster. 'Weapon?'

'Looks like an open razor,' Andrews said. 'Clean cuts, going deep. It looks like he lived for quite a few minutes after being left for dead.'

Taggart stooped down to examine Barrow's injuries more closely. He looked back down the stairs at the trail of blood. 'With his throat gashed like that?' he asked in disbelief.

Andrews shrugged. 'He had kids, Jim,' he said by way of explanation. 'It's often quite uncanny what reserves we can dredge up when our children are in danger.'

Taggart turned back to Jackie Reid. 'Who was he? Do we know anything about him yet?'

'Apparently he was a private detective, sir.'

Taggart raised his eyebrows. He glanced around the large and expensively furnished house. 'A private detective — with an au pair, and all this? In Bearsden?'

'Not just *any* private detective, sir. Tom Barrow was probably one of the three top investigators in Scotland. He did a lot of corporate work. Big money jobs.'

Taggart looked a little peeved. 'Nice work if you can get it,' he observed, realising a little belatedly that the comment was in particularly bad taste.

Apart from a throbbing headache, Jardine didn't feel too bad. He had waived the invitation to stay overnight in the hospital for observation, accepting a dose of mild painkillers instead. It was important that he talked to the only witness as soon as possible, while events, painful as they were, were still fresh in Simon's mind.

It would not be a pleasant task, Jardine reminded himself. He regarded the boy with a serious but friendly expression.

'Now, Simon. I know this isn't going to be easy for you, but I have to ask you some questions about your father and what you saw. Do you understand?'

Simon sat in front of a warm log fire with a borrowed adult dressing-gown draped over him. He seemed surprisingly calm, Jardine thought, although it was possible that the shock had not fully registered yet.

The boy nodded, his face sad but composed.

'I'm what Dad would call a material witness,' he said quietly. 'He said it was always important for witnesses to try and stay as calm and objective as possible.'

Jardine gave him a faint, reassuring smile. 'He was a very sensible man, your dad. Did you know much about the work he did, Simon?'

The boy nodded. 'We talked about it a lot. I want to be a detective when I grow up. Just like him.' He paused, a look of concern crossing his face. 'How's your head?'

Jardine rubbed the large bump on the back of his skull gently. 'Okay, I think. Hard heads run in my family. My dad was a policeman, too.'

'Anyway, Dad did mainly business and commercial work,' Simon went on. 'He said that's where the money was. He used to work in the Serious Fraud Office before he went private.'

'Do you know where he went last night? What he was working on?' Jardine asked.

'It was a missing person case. It was unusual, because he didn't do many of those. A businessman called Phillip Chalmers

32

from Edinburgh. I looked at the file before Dad went out last night.'

'Where's your mother, Simon?' Jardine asked gently.

Simon's eyes dropped to the floor. 'She's dead. She died about two years ago. That's why we have Agnetha.'

'Any aunts or uncles — grandparents?'

The boy shook his head sadly. 'There was only us and Dad.' He looked up at Jardine again, his eyes suddenly blazing with defiance. 'I want to help look for the person that killed him.'

Jardine nodded understandingly. 'And you can help, Simon. You can help us a great deal by describing the person who attacked your father.'

Simon thought for a few seconds. 'I didn't see his face,' he admitted. 'It was in shadow, and he had the hood of this rainmac pulled right over his head.'

'What colour was it?' Jardine asked.

'Blue. Dark blue, I think.'

'And the type of rainmac? Was it the sort that drapes over you, or the kind where you put your arms through the sleeve holes?'

Simon's face clouded over. He stared down at the floor as though ashamed that he couldn't remember.

Jardine reached forward and patted the boy gently on the back. 'It's all right, Simon. Don't worry. You were very brave — and you did save your little sister.'

'But I really want to help. I want to be a good detective,' Simon blurted out, his voice starting to break.

He was on the verge of bursting into tears, Jardine realised. He glanced at his watch, noting that it was almost 1.30 in the morning. The boy desperately needed rest after his terrifying ordeal.

'Look, Simon — what you need right now is a good night's sleep,' he told him. 'You're going to stay here tonight, with your neighbours, and tomorrow we'll sort out a nice temporary foster home for you and your sister.'

Simon nodded dumbly. He hadn't even considered the

problem of having somewhere to live. Or, indeed, the fact that he was now an orphan.

Chapter Four

Agnetha was calmer now, after a night of heavily sedated sleep. She faced Taggart and Jackie Reid with a frank, perfectly innocent expression on her pretty face.

'I sleep until I hear the crash. Then I wake up and go outside and find Mr Barrow,' she recounted, summing up events up to the time of the murder. She looked at Jackie, a slight frown creasing her face. 'What happen to me now?'

'Whereabouts in Sweden are you from, Agnetha?' Jackie asked.

'Finland,' the girl answered in all innocence.

Jackie repressed a smile. 'Sorry, it's been a long night for all of us. Where in Finland?'

'A place called Grankulla. Near Helsinki.'

'And how long have you worked for the family?' Taggart asked.

'Two years. Since Mrs Barrow die.'

Taggart cleared his throat, feeling a little awkward. 'Agnetha, I'm sorry I have to ask you personal questions —

but what was the relationship between you and Mr Barrow?'

Agnetha regarded him with a blank expression. 'Pardon?'

'Your relationship,' Taggart repeated. He glanced sideways at Jackie Reid, appealing for help.

'I was the au pair,' Agnetha said in answer to the last question.

Jackie came to the aid of her embarrassed superior.

'Were you any more than just the au pair?' she asked the girl.

Agnetha still looked as if she didn't understand what they were both driving at. 'I take children to school. I clean house. I cook meals. You want to know what else?'

Jackie looked sideways at Taggart, who shrugged. Either there was a language barrier or the girl was naïve in the extreme.

Suddenly Agnetha seemed to understand. Her face brightened. 'You mean — do we screw?' she asked. 'No — never.' She was quite adamant.

Taggart flashed a look of thanks at Jackie who smiled back at him.

'So you see, sir — it's not true what they say about Scandinavian girls.'

Taggart grunted noncommittally, rising to his feet. 'I'll leave you two babes in the wood together, then. I'm going to see McVitie.'

Jardine dropped a typed sheet on to Superintendent McVitie's desk.

'That's all we know about Tom Barrow, sir. Born in Yorkshire, ex-CID, joined the Serious Fraud Squad in London, eventually resigned after being passed over for promotion. He and his family moved to Glasgow seven years ago where he's done very lucrative private work. A very reliable and dedicated man of high principles, according to several of his clients.'

McVitie rubbed his chin reflectively. 'A private detective?

Then any one of his jobs might possibly have provided a motive.'

'There is the current case he was working on, sir,' Taggart put in. 'An unusual one, or so it seems. A missing person — one Phillip Chalmers, from Edinburgh. Managing director of Horfeldt Agricultural Equipment. It's a Dutch-British consortium.'

'Is he on our records?' McVitie wanted to know.

Taggart nodded. 'He went missing on a business trip here in Glasgow about two months ago. His car was found abandoned down near Jamaica Bridge.'

'Is it relevant, do you think?' McVitie asked.

'It could be, sir,' Jardine cut in. 'Barrow was definitely working on the case on the night of his murder. Both his son and the au pair confirm that he had a file marked "Phillip Chalmers" with him when he left the house. Now it isn't anywhere in the house, or in his car.'

'So, as it's highly unlikely that he left it somewhere, we assume that the murderer took it,' Taggart said, finishing off.

'And you are also assuming a connection?' McVitie seemed a little dubious.

'It makes sense, sir,' Taggart said, feeling slightly on the defensive.

McVitie chose not to pursue the matter any further. 'What's happening to the children?'

'Emergency foster parents, sir,' Jardine informed him. 'DC Reid and I are taking them there as soon as this briefing is over.'

McVitie nodded understandingly. 'Well, you'd better get going then,' he said kindly. 'The sooner those unfortunate children get someone to look after them the better.'

Seen from the road outside, the Old Merchant House did not look at all welcoming. In fact, it looked positively forbidding, Jardine thought. He cast a sideways, dubious glance at Jackie

Reid, sitting in the passenger seat beside him.

Almost as if picking up his thoughts, Nicola piped up from the back seat in a frightened, unhappy little voice. 'I don't like it. It looks creepy. I want to go home.'

Jackie turned round in her seat, attempting to comfort the child. 'You can't go home just yet, Nicola. This will only be for a few days. Besides, I expect the people inside will be really nice.'

The child was unconvinced. She clung to her brother, needing reassurance that he was unable to give her. Simon too thought the gaunt house looked cold and unfriendly.

'Come on — I expect it's really nice inside,' Jardine said, trying to sound positive. He got out of the car and opened the back door, helping the children out as Jackie gathered their emergency clothes together.

He led the way up the long path to the front door, Simon and Nicola trailing reluctantly behind him.

The front door opened as they reached it. William and Jessie Frazer stood side by side in the doorway. Jardine thought that they looked curiously like two carved figures in an old-fashioned weather-house. Mr Rain and Mrs Sunshine: William Frazer, a tall, cadaverous-looking individual, and Jessie, a short, slight, almost bird-like little woman. Still, they both had warm smiles of welcome on their faces, which was something.

Jardine opened his mouth to make the introductions, but Frazer pre-empted him. 'You must be Simon and Nicola,' he said to the children. 'We've been looking out for you. I'm Mr Frazer and this is Mrs Frazer. We want you both to feel very much at home here.'

He stepped back into the hallway of the house, bidding them welcome to enter. Nicola shrank back, clutching at Jackie Reid's hand. Simon merely stood his ground, saying nothing.

Frazer seemed to understand. 'You've both been through a terrible and tragic experience,' he said gently. 'Now, please — do come in and Mrs Frazer will show you to your rooms.'

Jardine nudged Simon over the threshold, whilst Jackie tugged in the unwilling Nicola. Frazer led Jardine through the large, bare hallway towards the living area as his wife took Jackie and the children upstairs. 'We can talk in the library,' he said.

Jardine followed him, increasingly aware that the interior of the house was much like the outside — old-fashioned and cold-looking. Although the Frazers seemed friendly enough, he couldn't help thinking that the Social Service Department could have come up with something better, considering the circumstances.

Frazer walked into the wood-panelled library and sat down on an old leather chair. He looked up at Jardine with the air of a schoolmaster admonishing an errant pupil.

'I want you to leave the children here alone for a few days,' he said. 'Give them a chance to settle in and adjust after all they've been through. Is that clear?'

Jardine was slightly taken aback by the man's attitude. 'The boy witnessed his father's murder. We may need to talk to him again,' he pointed out.

Frazer shook his head. 'No, that's out of the question. They both need time,' he said firmly. He rose from the chair as though, having given his instructions, the matter was settled. 'Now, unless there's anything you think you should tell me . . .'

Jardine was speechless. Before he fully realised it Frazer had escorted him back to the front door and was virtually ejecting him over the threshold. He stood outside on the path until Jackie came out.

'Strange pair,' he muttered as Frazer closed the front door with an air of finality. They began to walk down the path towards the car. Jackie stopped, suddenly, turning to look back at the house.

'Nicola was right,' she said after some thought. 'It is creepy.'

Taggart's phone rang. He snatched up the receiver, answering brusquely. 'Taggart.'

The voice on the other end had a suave, deliberately cultured Edinburgh accent. 'Detective Chief Inspector Bobby Gault here. Edinburgh CID. I understand there could be a connection between a missing Edinburgh man and your recent murder.'

Taggart was instantly on his guard. He had an instinctive distrust of other police forces, along with a somewhat cynical opinion of Edinburgh folk and their high-falutin, superior ways.

'Could be,' he said, giving nothing away.

'It occurred to me that I might be able to help you with some facts,' Gault went on. 'Let's just say that there are some suspicious circumstances, although they don't really suggest murder.'

Taggart bristled at the man's patronising attitude. 'Then I'd better come and find what they *do* suggest,' he snapped. He slammed the telephone back into its cradle rather abruptly and stormed out into the outer office.

Jackie Reid and Jardine had just returned from the Frazer house.

'Don't bother taking off your coat,' Taggart told her. 'You're driving me to Edinburgh.'

Jackie gave him her most put-upon expression. 'Do I have a choice, sir?' she asked, knowing the answer before she phrased the question. With a faint shrug in Jardine's direction, she turned and followed Taggart out of the office.

Gault's office could have passed for that of a senior executive in some multinational corporation. Taggart glowered at the finely polished beech desk, the sculptured easy chairs and the richly piled carpet. His chagrin was increased by the arrival of a WPC with a tea-tray laden with biscuits, cream cakes and paper doilies, which she proceeded to lay out on the desk as if serving a banquet. Smiling sweetly, she distributed bone china cups and departed.

Gault held the china teapot elegantly in one hand, preparing to pour. 'I hope you don't mind Earl Grey?' he enquired solicitously.

Taggart glanced sideways at Jackie Reid, who looked as amazed as he was. He grinned. 'Oh, no. We drink it all the time in the station canteen.'

Gault ignored the obvious sarcasm and poured the tea. He lounged back in his chair, producing a silver cigarette case from his pocket with something of a flourish. 'I do hope you don't mind if I smoke.'

Without waiting for any possible objections, Gault opened the cigarette case and drew out a gold-tipped, bright green cocktail cigarette, holding it delicately between his fingers and lighting it.

Taggart watched him with a mounting sense of disbelief as he sucked on the cigarette, threw back his head and plumed a thin stream of smoke into the air.

'As you know, it's not a crime to go missing,' he said eventually. 'Phillip Chalmers may have chosen to do a Reggie Perrin, for all we know.'

'You said there were suspicious circumstances,' Taggart reminded him.

Gault took another exaggerated drag on the cigarette and nodded faintly. 'The thing is, I knew Phillip Chalmers. Only socially, of course,' he hastened to add. 'We belonged to the same lodge.'

'Did he seem the type to go missing voluntarily?' Taggart cut in before Gault launched into a listing of his club memberships and charity donations.

The DCI gave an affected shrug of his shoulders. 'Who can tell what goes on in a man's mind? All I can tell you is that he telephoned his wife on the day he disappeared. From a phone-box in Glasgow.'

'Any message?' Taggart wanted to know.

'He told her he loved her,' Gault said. 'And that he'd be back about ten that evening. He never did return, of course.'

'How did he sound — when he made the call?'

'Perfectly normal, I understand.'

'And money?' Taggart prompted. 'What did he have on him when he disappeared?'

'His cheque-book, of course. The usual credit cards. We know he drew out sixty pounds on the day he disappeared. And the clothes he stood up in,' Gault answered.

'No subsequent drawings on his account, I take it.'

Gault shook his head. 'Nothing. It's a joint account with his wife.' He broke off to stub out his half-smoked cigarette in the ashtray and select a cream cake. 'Being a joint account, it's frozen, of course,' he continued. 'People who disappear leave a lot of problems like that.'

Jackie Reid watched Gault nibble delicately at his cake. Taking it as an open invitation, she helped herself to a biscuit.

'Oh, there's another strange fact,' Gault said suddenly, as though he had just remembered. 'When Chalmers' wife retrieved his car, she found cake crumbs on the driving seat.'

Jackie paused, the biscuit only halfway to her mouth. 'Why is that strange?'

'Phillip had recently had a blood cholesterol test and the reading was high. He was on a strict diet,' Gault informed her.

'We all break diets, sir,' Jackie said, taking a large bite out of her biscuit.

'Perhaps he was so worried about his health that he committed suicide,' Taggart put in.

Gault looked at him with faint disapproval, regarding the remark as flippant. 'Anyway, there's really not much else I can tell you.'

Taggart started to rise from his chair. 'Well, if we're finished here, I'd like to go and talk to Chalmers' wife.'

'Oh, you can't do that,' Gault said. 'She's on holiday at present.'

Taggart's mouth dropped open in disbelief. He sank back into his chair. 'Her husband is missing, she hires a private detective — and then she goes on holiday?' he muttered incredulously. He stared at Gault closely, as though seeking some sort of explanation. The man merely looked back at him, his face impassive.

He was hiding something, Taggart was sure. It was more than a hunch, it was a gut feeling.

Chapter Five

Jackie Reid was recounting her Edinburgh trip to Jardine as they searched through the Barrow house for any clues which might have been overlooked.

'And you should have seen the boss's face when he lit up a green cigarette,' she said. 'I thought he was going to have a fit.'

Jardine grinned broadly, picturing the scene. 'Green? I can just imagine his face.'

'I think he thought it was all part of some bizarre Edinburgh tea-drinking ritual,' Jackie said, laughing. 'Anyway, then Gault told him that Chalmers' wife was away on a Nile cruise or something and he almost blew a fuse.'

Jardine picked up the leather-bound book of *Grimm's Fairy Tales* from Simon's bed. It fell open at the most frequently read page. Jardine looked down at the picture of the princess in the flowing blue cape, the smile fading from his face.

'Here, look at this,' he murmured, drawing Jackie's attention to the illustration.

She studied the caped and hooded figure carefully for a few seconds, finally looking up to meet the questioning look in Jardine's eyes.

'Coincidence?' she suggested.

Jardine wasn't sure. He closed the book, tucking it under his arm. 'Let's go and find out.'

Jessie Frazer regarded Jardine and Jackie with open disapproval as she opened the door.

'We've just come to see Simon,' Jackie said with a friendly smile.

It was not returned. 'Oh, I don't think so,' Jessie murmured. 'He's having his dinner. And besides, I think it's too soon to bother him after all he's been through . . . don't you?'

She began to close the door in their faces. Jardine stepped forward, putting his foot over the threshold and jamming it.

'This is a murder inquiry, Mrs Frazer,' he reminded her forcefully. He waved the book in the air. 'Anyway, we mainly came to give him this.'

'I'll give it to him.' Jessie held out her hand for the book.

'Don't bother. We'll do it,' Jackie said sweetly, treading over Jardine's foot and neatly side-stepping the woman. Jardine followed her into the house, walking down the hallway towards the library.

Looking extremely disgruntled, Jessie Frazer scuttled off to fetch her husband.

Jackie smiled at Jardine. 'It was probably easier getting into Spandau,' she murmured.

Frazer stormed into the library, his face angry. 'I understand you've come to see Simon again,' he said, accusingly. 'I thought I made it quite clear that I didn't want him disturbed for a few days.'

'It's all right. I'm here,' Simon said from behind him. He walked into the library, giving Jardine a faint smile.

Jardine held out the book. 'I thought you might want this.'

45

'Thanks.' Simon held out his hand gratefully. Taking the book he hugged it against his body like the treasured possession it was.

'A special book, is it?' Jardine asked.

Simon nodded proudly. 'It's a rare edition. My dad gave it to me for my seventh birthday.'

Jardine paused, choosing his words carefully. 'Simon, there's a picture in that book — a princess, in a blue cape,' he said quietly.

The boy's eyes clouded over with guilt. 'What about it?' he said guardedly.

'It's just that . . . the clothes she's wearing . . . the blue cape with the hood. That's almost exactly what you described to me last night,' Jardine pointed out. He waited for a reaction.

Simon regarded him blankly, failing to see the point of the observation.

Jardine sighed, feeling a trifle awkward. 'Look, Simon — are you absolutely *sure* that's what you saw?' he asked finally, unable to put it any more subtly.

Simon's eyes blazed defiantly. 'I'm sure. Why, don't you believe me?'

'Of course we believe you, Simon,' Jackie said gently. 'Anyway, you can keep the book now, if you want.'

'And my bike? Could I have that as well?'

Jardine nodded. 'We'll have it sent round,' he promised.

'Right, if that's all settled, then perhaps Simon can go back and finish his dinner,' Frazer said firmly. He moved in protectively, shooing the boy out of the room. He looked across at Jardine. 'I think children have childhood taken away far too soon these days,' he said curiously.

Jardine cast a puzzled glance at Jackie, who merely shrugged. She didn't understand the significance of the remark either.

Taggart brought Superintendent McVitie up to date with the

day's events. There wasn't much to tell. McVitie looked vexed.

'Twenty-four hours and we've neither a suspect nor a single clue. Have you no leads at all?'

Taggart shook his head. 'Nothing, sir.'

'What about the au pair?' McVitie asked.

She had nothing to do with it, sir. I'm certain of it,' Taggart said firmly. 'Besides, she was already inside the house when the boy saw the murderer enter.'

'But we can't be sure that the boy really did see what he says he saw,' McVitie pointed out. 'He could have imagined it all, for all we know. The whole experience must have been unbelievably traumatic for him. Nor do we know that Barrow's death is in any way connected with this Chalmers case.'

'But something smells about it, sir,' Taggart insisted.

McVitie was not convinced. 'A wife goes on holiday. After two months of strain, perhaps she needed the rest. Listen, Jim — I don't want us going up that road to the exclusion of all the other cases Barrow worked on. There could be something else there.'

Taggart conceded the point reluctantly. It was that old gut-feeling again, telling him that he was on the right track with the Chalmers connection. 'All right, sir — I'll put a couple of people on to it first thing in the morning.'

It seemed to satisfy his superior. McVitie nodded and turned his attention back to the paperwork on his desk.

Chapter Six

Simon lay in bed in a light fitful sleep which hovered between waking, sleep and nightmare. In his conscious moments he was aware of the sound of rain outside lashing against the bedroom window. Then the insistent, hypnotic sound would send him drifting off again, back in time to a better place, a better day.

Nicola, skipping through the bushes, chuckling happily, the big jug of blackberries in her hand. The late autumn sunshine shafting down through the trees above his head, playing on the dappled leaves beneath his feet. His father, crouched on one knee and looking up at him with that proud smile on his face.

'Well spotted, son. There must be a sett nearby. Well spotted, son. Well spotted . . . well spotted . . . well spotted.'

Then the smile turning to a look of shocked horror. The whistling, slashing sound of the cut-throat razor. The blood. Terror — terror and disbelief.

'Well spotted, son. You'll make a fine detective.'

The nightmares lasted only momentarily before shock jolted Simon back into the present and a state of semi-wakefulness, listening to the sound of the rain beating against the bedroom window. And the cycle began again, reinforcing the subliminal message in Simon's brain. His father was telling him he had to be a detective. He had to know the identity of the killer in the blue cape. Until then, there was no time for tears, no room for grief. No time, in fact, to even confront the full horror of what he had seen.

A waking moment came round again, but there was a new factor to change the cycle. Above the noise of the rain, Simon was aware of the sound of a car door slamming outside the front of the house. Then hurried footsteps running up the path towards the front door.

Simon threw back his bed covers and got out of bed, now fully awake. He moved to the bedroom door, opening it and stepping out on to the landing. Reaching the banister railings, he peered through them down into the large lobby on the ground floor, having a clear view of the front door.

Jessie Frazer was already on her way to open it, even though the bell had not rung. Obviously, it was somebody she had been expecting. She opened the door and stepped back into the lobby, welcoming the visitor into the house.

Upstairs, Simon's knuckles whitened as he gripped the banister rails tightly, his whole body tensing as a figure in a dark blue rain cape and hood stepped into the house and strode swiftly across the lobby towards the drawing-room.

Gemma waited for Jardine in the police station reception area. Partly to kill time, and partly in the line of research, she was reading the noticeboard. One particular old poster caught her attention. It had obviously been there for some time. Gemma looked at the deceptively innocent face of the man in the photograph, which seemed oddly out of keeping with the message printed prominently beneath it.

WANTED
IN CONNECTION WITH A SERIES OF MURDERS
IN THE STRATHCLYDE AREA
WARNING: DO NOT APPROACH

Gemma was unaware of Jardine coming up behind her. His voice, coming unexpectedly in her ear, made her jump slightly.

'That's the only one we never caught. More than likely sunning himself on some beach in Brazil.'

Gemma turned, grasping his arm. 'The one who got away, eh? Maybe I'll leave him out.'

Jardine failed to understand. 'Leave him out of what?'

'Oh, didn't I tell you? My next book is going to be an anthology of Glasgow murders. The Glasgow Bowman, the Balfour case, the Samson murder.'

'I worked on the Bowman case,' Jardine put in. 'In fact, it was me that discovered the clue which eventually led us to him.'

Gemma looked impressed. 'That's great! You'll have to tell me all about it.'

'Some other time,' Jardine said, smiling. 'Right now I'm finished for the day and I'm taking you out for the evening. The last thing I plan to do is to talk shop.'

He slid his arm around her waist. 'So, what's it to be? Chinese, Indian — or do you fancy the Italian touch? There's a rather nice new pizzaria not too far away from here. Cheap and cheerful — but you're dating a copper, not a bestselling author.'

Gemma had already turned towards the exit. 'I think dinner is going to have to wait,' she announced. 'You seem to have a visitor.'

With something of a sinking feeling Jardine turned round to confront the dripping, shivering figure of Simon who stood just inside the doorway, waiting for him. The boy looked extremely agitated Jardine realised.

He glanced sideways at Gemma, an apologetic look on his face. 'Do you mind an extra guest for dinner?' he asked.

The pizzaria was quite crowded. Jardine found a spare table, made sure that Gemma and Simon were seated, and nodded over towards a pay phone on the far wall.

'I'd better go and telephone the Frazers to tell them we've found you,' he muttered to Simon. 'They'll probably be worried about you.'

The boy seemed to have calmed down somewhat by the time he returned. He sat sipping at a glass of Coke which Gemma had ordered for him. Jardine sat down.

'The person you saw at the Frazers' house tonight was Mrs Frazer's brother,' he told Simon. 'He's a children's entertainer, a magician. Certainly nothing sinister about him. He lives in the house, in a converted flat behind the main building.'

'Well, there was obviously something about him that frightened Simon,' Gemma said. She had been watching the boy's face carefully while Jardine had been making the phone call. He was obviously very disturbed.

'I wasn't frightened,' Simon muttered defiantly. 'It was the same blue mac and hood.'

'Simon, there must be hundreds of people out there with similar raincoats,' Jardine pointed out. 'And it is raining.'

The boy seemed to accept this explanation reluctantly, but he was still defiant. 'Anyway, I don't like it in that house. And it frightens Nicola.'

Jardine fixed him with a firm look. 'Well, you're going straight back there when you've had something to eat.' He raised a hand to summon the waitress who was just passing the table. 'Could we have two Veneziana, please?"

The waitress scribbled on her pad. 'And what would your son like?'

Simon chipped in with his order before Jardine could correct the misunderstanding. 'I'll have a Four Seasons with extra pepperoni.'

Jardine glanced across at Gemma. 'Sorry, but I seem to have landed you with a family already.'

She smiled. 'Actually, you'd probably make a very good dad,' she murmured.

Jardine wasn't sure whether to take it as a compliment or not. Slightly embarrassed, he was silent until the food arrived.

There was no trace of recrimination on Frazer's face as he opened the door and looked down at Simon. Jardine pushed him gently into the house. The boy stood in the doorway, reluctant to leave him.

'Thanks for bringing him back,' Frazer said. 'We had no idea he'd sneaked out.'

Jardine shrugged. 'Just try to make sure that he doesn't run away again.'

Frazer began to close the door. Jardine was acutely aware of Simon's eyes upon him until the very last second. He suddenly seemed much more vulnerable — a lost, hurt and extremely lonely little boy.

'It must feel awful,' Jardine said to Gemma as they walked back down the garden path towards the car. 'Uprooted like that and suddenly thrust into a house full of strangers.'

'He seems extraordinarily well adjusted,' Gemma observed. 'Considering what he's been through.'

Jardine nodded thoughtfully. In fact, he had been slightly worried about Simon's reactions all along. 'Children do cope with trauma in different ways,' he murmured. 'In Simon's case, I don't think the shock has quite hit him yet. I'm not sure what will happen when it finally does.'

Gemma looked impressed. 'I didn't know you were an expert on child psychology as well.'

Jardine grinned sheepishly. 'Hardly an expert. I used to

work with a lot of kids doing community youth work. You get to understand them a little more — especially the disturbed ones.'

They had reached the car. Jardine opened the passenger door and helped Gemma into her seat. 'Well, so much for our evening out, or what's left of it. I'd better drive you home, I suppose.'

Gemma looked up at him, a roguish twinkle in her brown eyes. 'Can we go the long route . . . remember?'

Jardine smiled. He remembered only too well — as though it were only yesterday.

Albert Brockwell stood to greet Simon as Frazer ushered him into the drawing-room. He was well into his sixties, with a grizzled grey beard and the slight stoop of age to his gait. But his eyes carried a bright sparkle which belied his years, and the warmth of his smile was genuine enough.

'Simon, this is Mr Brockwell, my brother,' Jessie Frazer said.

Brockwell extended his hand. 'So this is the young man with the over-active imagination.' He stared deeply into Simon's eyes. 'Shall I tell you something about imagination, Simon? It's a rare and very precious gift.'

Brockwell waved his hand in the air. Simon was slightly startled and stepped back warily. He had been expecting the man to shake his hand. Instead, Brockwell performed a series of graceful manoeuvres, culminating in a grand flourish. To Simon's delight and amazement a white dove appeared as if from nowhere and flew twice around the room before finally alighting on the old man's shoulder.

'Do you know what the white dove is a symbol of, Simon?' Brockwell asked him gently.

Simon nodded. 'Peace.'

'Quite right.' Brockwell smiled warmly. 'Now, do you still think I mean you some sort of harm?'

Simon shook his head apologetically. Jessie Frazer looked

relieved. She placed her hands gently on Simon's shoulders, steering him towards the door. 'Now, off to bed with you. It's very late.'

The old parking spot was still there, Jardine was relieved to find. He pulled off the road into the narrow, rutted lane and drove up to the grassy area at the top of the hill. Switching off the engine and lights, he looked sideways out of the window at the twinkling lights of the city spread out below.

He relaxed back in his seat. 'It hardly seems to have changed at all,' he said to Gemma, the faintest trace of surprise in his voice.

Gemma snuggled up close to him. 'There is one thing which has changed,' she pointed out, nodding to a large wooden sign just in front of the car. 'That sign wasn't there eighteen years ago.'

Jardine looked at it, just able to read the wording in the gloom.

PRIVATE LAND
NO DUMPING
NO TRESPASSING
NO COURTING COUPLES

'Shall I get out and tear it down?' he offered recklessly.

Gemma smiled. 'Such lawlessness,' she chided jokingly. She raised her head slightly, inviting a kiss.

They kissed, with mounting passion, for some time. Finally, Gemma pulled back slightly and cast a furtive glance at her watch.

'You never worried about the time in the old days,' Jardine joked, noticing.

Gemma looked at him apologetically. 'Sorry, Mike. It's Mum and Dad. They'll be waiting up for me, I know it.'

'Still?' Jardine was surprised.

Gemma grinned. 'They're wonderful really, but I don't think they ever got over the shock of me not being sixteen any more.'

'I remember the time I took you home at four in the morning,' Jardine recalled.

'That's probably what traumatised them. It's your fault, you see,' Gemma told him.

'Do they let you do any work?' Jardine asked. There was a wild idea forming in his mind.

Gemma frowned slightly. 'No, not really,' she admitted. 'Mum brings me cups of tea every ten minutes and Dad keeps moving the standard lamp just a little nearer to the table. They're both well meaning, but a bit over-protective. But it's only a temporary measure, until I can find a place of my own.'

It was the very introduction that Jardine had been hoping for. Impulsively, he gripped Gemma by the shoulders. 'Look, I've got a better idea, Why don't you move in with me for a while?'

Gemma's initial reaction was of half-joking rejection. 'I wouldn't get *any* writing done then.'

Jardine shook his head. 'No, seriously. With the hours I work, you'd hardly ever see me. You'd have the place to yourself all day and probably most evenings. It would be ideal.'

His words made sense. Gemma gave the proposition a few moments of serious consideration. The more she thought about it, the more attractive it became. Finally, she nodded her head.

'Okay — it's a deal,' she said.

Jardine's heart leapt. He pulled her against him, hugging her passionately. His lips crushed against hers.

Suddenly there was a loud, urgent tapping on the wind-screen, and a bright light illuminated the interior of the car.

Jardine looked up in shock to see a uniformed police officer peering into the car with a large flashlight in his hand.

Beside him Gemma dissolved into girlish laughter.
Jardine was not amused.

Chapter Seven

Taggart stood in the garden, sipping his morning cup of tea and watching his wife prune back the rose-bushes from her wheelchair. He regarded her thoughtfully.

'If I disappeared suddenly, what would you do?' he blurted out, voicing the question which had been nagging at him for some time.

'You're forever disappearing suddenly,' Jean Taggart responded, refusing to take the question seriously.

Her husband frowned with exasperation. 'No, I mean — if I *really* disappeared. Like for weeks, or months, and you had no idea where I was. How would you react?'

Jean could see that he was serious. She considered the possibility for a second, finally giving him a faint shrug. 'I don't know. Just try to get on with living, I suppose.'

Taggart looked shell-shocked. 'You wouldn't even report me missing?' he asked incredulously.

'Well, of course I'd report you missing,' Jean told him, wondering what he was actually trying to get at.

'And how long would you sit by the phone? Waiting for news of me?' Taggart went on.

'That depends.'

'Depends on what?'

'On whether I thought you were ever coming home or not.'

Taggart sighed with exasperation. 'Well, how long would it be before you, say, went off on holiday? Took a break?'

Jean thought for a moment. 'Oh, I don't know. Six weeks, two months, maybe.'

Taggart's face had the look of a forlorn little boy. 'Six weeks, two months,' he repeated pathetically. 'Thanks.' He finished his tea and began to walk back into the house.

Jean turned from the roses for the first time and watched his departing back. 'Didn't I give you the answers you wanted?' she called after him.

Taggart didn't turn round. 'I'll see you tonight. I'm off to Edinburgh,' he muttered.

DCI Gault was waiting in the crescent-shaped drive of the Chalmers house when Taggart arrived with Jackie Reid. He leaned nonchalantly against the side of his car, smoking a bright yellow cigarette.

'She's on her way from the airport now,' Gault announced as Taggart walked over. 'She should be here at any moment.' He glanced up the street as a taxi slowed down on its approach to the house, its indicator blinking. 'In fact, this could be her now.'

The taxi pulled into the drive. The driver got out, unloading several suitcases before opening the passenger door. A pair of slim and elegant legs swung out, and Elsa Chalmers emerged.

She was, Taggart had to concede, a very beautiful and striking woman, with the elegant bearing that only old money, good breeding and worldly sophistication could bring. She paid the taxi-driver and regarded her reception committee with cool disdain.

Gault stepped forward. 'Elsa, this is Detective Chief Inspector Taggart and DC Reid from Glasgow.'

The woman regarded him coolly. 'Have you found Phillip?' she asked, almost as casually as requesting directions to the nearest bank.

'No. Sorry,' Taggart said.

She looked more annoyed than disappointed, Taggart thought. 'Then why are you here?'

'It's about the private detective you hired to look for your husband,' Taggart told her. 'He's been murdered.'

He was deliberately blunt, wanting to see the woman's reaction. For the first time Taggart thought he noticed her composure crack slightly, although she covered it up well.

'Well, I suppose you'd better come into the house,' Elsa said, turning and walking towards the front door. She left the suitcases on the drive, obviously assuming that the two men would carry them in for her.

She showed them into an elegantly furnished lounge and sat down on one of the armchairs, crossing her knees. 'I spoke to Mr Barrow just before I left. I told him that if he made any important discoveries he could contact me abroad.'

'When was that?' Taggart asked.

Elsa thought for a moment. 'It must have been two weeks yesterday. He drove over here, I made him lunch and we talked about Phillip. I gave him all the recent photographs I had.'

'Do you know what angles he intended to work on?' Jackie Reid asked.

Elsa shook her head. 'No, I don't. Only that as his car was found in Glasgow, someone might have seen him. Other than that, I have no idea of where he intended to look.' She glanced at Gault, as though seeking reassurance. 'Look, you don't think Mr Barrow's death has anything to do with Phillip, do you?'

'We don't know,' Gault said gently. 'But there could be a connection.'

'I just want to know whether he's committed suicide or whether he's washing dishes somewhere in Glasgow suffering from amnesia,' Elsa said, turning her attention back to Taggart. 'Apparently some men do that — they just forget who they are and adopt new identities.'

'And some men just don't want to be found,' Taggart added. 'Was he under any particular pressure? Financial, or company problems?'

Elsa shook her head emphatically. 'Certainly not. The company was doing very well, and we haven't any money worries.'

'What about emotional pressures?' Taggart suggested. 'Were there any other women in his life?'

Again, Elsa was adamant. 'No.'

'How can you be sure of that?' Taggart demanded.

Elsa shrugged faintly. 'I can't be *sure*, of course, but I just know.'

'Did you have any kind of a row the day he disappeared? Or had you been having any personal problems?'

The faintest shadow of doubt flickered briefly across Elsa Chalmers' face. This time her answer was more guarded. 'Phillip had no reason for wanting to disappear that I know of. He telephoned me to say that he loved me on the day he went missing. This was the last thing I heard from him.'

Jackie Reid tried another angle. 'Did Mr Chalmers have any enemies? Anyone with a motive or reason for wishing him dead?'

Elsa Chalmers looked at her dismissively. 'Phillip was a charming, gentle man. Of course no one would want to kill him.'

Taggart rose to his feet. The interview was producing nothing. 'Mrs Chalmers, if Tom Barrow had come up with anything while you were away, how was he supposed to get in touch with you?'

'Why, through the travel company, of course.' Elsa got up to show them to the door.

'Did you enjoy the cruise, by the way?' Taggart asked sarcastically as he was leaving.

Elsa Chalmers failed to see the sarcasm. 'Oh, yes, the Nile was lovely,' she answered with a perfectly straight face.

'Well, what do you make of that?' Taggart asked Jackie Reid as they walked towards the car.

Jackie grinned faintly. 'Bit like "if anything important comes up at the office, let me know, otherwise it can wait until I get back".'

Taggart nodded. 'That's the impression I got.'

Gault paused by his car to light up a red cigarette. 'Don't you think you're both reading too much into it?' he asked.

'No,' Taggart said flatly.

'She has dignity,' Gault said, appearing to defend her. 'She doesn't want to be seen weeping and wailing.' He climbed into his car and started the engine, winding down the window. 'I'd appreciate it if you'd contact me first, if you want anything else.'

He drove off, leaving Taggart staring after him thoughtfully. There was something about the man he didn't trust, and it had nothing to do with him smoking coloured cigarettes. But for the moment it was too vague to be of any real use. Turning back towards their own car he called over to Jackie, who was admiring the impressive façade of the Chalmers' house. 'Come on, let's get back to the real world.'

They were just driving off when the front door of the house flew open and Elsa Chalmers ran out into the drive, waving her arms in a very agitated fashion. She shouted after the departing car. 'Stop!'

Jackie saw her in the rear-view mirror and stamped on the brakes. The car slewed to a halt in the gravel of the drive.

Elsa ran to the side of the car. Looking out at her, Taggart could see that her usually cool and composed features were quite distraught. She had obviously received a nasty shock.

Taggart unclipped his seat belt and jumped out of the car. 'What is it?'

Elsa Chalmers fought to compose herself. 'I went to check my answerphone tape after you left,' she blurted out. 'There's a message on it that I think you ought to hear.'

Taggart and Jackie Reid followed her back into the house, intrigued by what could possibly have flustered the woman this much. They were soon to find out.

Elsa led the way to the answerphone machine and set it to rewind. As the tape whirred back, she looked up at Taggart, her voice a little shaky.

'What you're going to hear is Tom Barrow's voice,' she told him. 'He sounds strange, horrible . . . and the message doesn't make any sense . . . but it's definitely him.'

The tape stopped playing back with a faint click. Elsa pressed the play button. There were a couple of short messages from female friends and then a longish pause.

'This is it now,' Elsa said and fell silent.

Tom Barrow's voice was broken and horribly distorted, thick and choking. 'Tell . . . them . . . check other . . . . missing . . . persons . . . Ginger . . . bread . . . Men.'

The message ended with a final sickening, gurgling, choking sound, then there was silence.

Taggart stopped the tape and cast a sideways look at Jackie Reid.

'That last phone call,' she breathed.

Taggart nodded. 'We wondered who it could have been that he tried to call. Now we know.'

Elsa Chalmers gaped at him with renewed horror on her face. 'You mean he was actually *dying* when he made that call?'

'Bleeding to death and with his throat slashed open,' Taggart muttered, his words meant more for Jackie than to increase Elsa Chalmers' discomfort. 'He must have thought that message was pretty important.'

Jackie nodded. 'But what does it mean? Gingerbread Men?'

'What indeed,' Taggart mused. The cryptic message didn't seem to make any sense at all.

He turned to Elsa. 'I'll have to take that tape, Mrs Chalmers.'

'Yes, of course.' Elsa slipped the cassette out of the machine and passed it to him hurriedly as though she couldn't wait to get it out of the house.

After Taggart left, Elsa Chalmers walked out of the lounge into the kitchen, looking extremely worried. Bobby Gault stood there, the faintest trace of concern on his face. After leaving Taggart he had driven straight around to the rear of the house and let himself in by the back door. For obvious reasons he had kept out of sight.

'You heard?' Elsa asked.

Gault nodded. He looked at Elsa with concern, seeing how shaken up she was. He lit two cigarettes, passing one to her. 'Don't worry, you handled things just fine,' he told her.

Elsa sucked on the yellow cigarette nervously. 'I'm worried, Bobby. It's getting too nasty, too complicated. Sooner or later they're going to find out why I hired Tom Barrow.'

Gault shook his head reassuringly. 'There's no reason why they should,' he said calmly. 'Let's just keep it to ourselves for as long as possible. At least until we know, one way or the other.'

Elsa wasn't totally convinced, but she tried to take his words at face value. Now that Phillip was gone, she had no one else to turn to.

Chapter Eight

Brockwell was dressed in his full stage magician outfit complete with old-fashioned dress-suit, high-winged collar, white gloves and a neatly waxed and curled moustache. He worked from an improvised stage erected on old packing cases in the lobby of the Frazer house, in front of a small but enthusiastic audience of young children invited from various orphanages and other foster homes in the vicinity.

Simon sat in the very back row, watching the performance with a fixed stare but with his mind elsewhere.

Brockwell was calling for a volunteer from the audience to be sawn in half. A dozen small hands went up, and several more of the children stood up on their seats, clamouring for attention.

Simon saw his chance and took it, getting up quietly from his chair and moving towards the front door as everyone's attention was focused on Brockwell and his fearsome-looking saw. Nobody noticed as he slipped out of the house and hurried round to the shed at the back where his bike was kept.

He climbed on it with a surging feeling of release in his heart, thankful to be out of the claustrophobic atmosphere of the house. He needed to be on his own for a while, close to his most recent memories of his father. Simon began to pedal away furiously, some instinctive urge taking him in the direction of Dunleath Woods and Betty Duncan's cottage.

He was exhausted when he finally arrived. Dropping his bike beneath a tree, Simon sat down beside it and picked a handful of blackberries from a nearby bush, cramming them into his mouth. He lay back against the trunk of the tree, closing his eyes against the bright sunlight which shafted down through the bare branches above his head.

As he had somehow known it would, the image of his father's gentle, happy face formed in his mind, Simon smiled dreamily, confident that this time there would be no nightmares. Sharing the discovery of the badger tracks with his father yet again, Simon dropped off into a light sleep.

The sound of a noisy, badly tuned car jerked him from his reverie. Sitting up, Simon watched the progress of a battered Ford Panda along the rough track which led to the cottage some two hundred yards away. The car stopped by the side of the cottage and a figure stepped out.

Squinting against the sunlight in his eyes, Simon stared at the indistinct and distant figure with a shiver of apprehension running through his body. Although it was only a matter of seconds before the occupant of the car had disappeared around the side of the cottage, there was no mistaking that blue cape and hood.

Shakily, Simon pushed himself to his feet and reached down for his bicycle. Jumping on to it he began to pedal as fast as he could across the rough forest ground.

Jardine sat perched on the corner of his desk, the telephone in his hand as he looked down at the seated Simon with an expression of faint exasperation on his face.

'Yes, he's here again,' Jardine muttered into the mouthpiece. 'But don't worry, I'll bring him back.'

He replaced the receiver, staring at Simon thoughtfully for a few seconds.

'Look, shall I give you some advice about being a detective, Simon? You need to have some imagination, but not too much.' Jardine paused, slightly puzzled. 'What were you doing in those woods, anyway?'

'Dad took us there, picking blackberries. The day before —' Simon broke off, unable or unwilling to finish the sentence.

There was a moment of silence, eventually broken by Taggart as he came out of his office. He looked over at the young boy. 'Are you here again, Simon?'

'Simon has seen another caped figure,' Jardine explained, a trifle wearily. 'This time at a cottage in Dunleath Woods.'

The disbelief in Jardine's tone was obvious. Simon jumped to his feet protesting vehemently. 'This time I'm certain. It was the same person! You've *got* to believe me.'

Taggart flashed Jardine a slightful doubtful glance. 'You'd better check it out.'

Jardine sighed. He was already convinced it would turn out to be another wild goose chase. He looked at Simon miserably. 'Come on, then. I'll drop you off on the way.'

The Fiat Panda was there, just as Simon had described it. Jardine took a furtive look inside before approaching the cottage door. Satisfied that it contained nothing of interest, he walked round the car quickly, checking the bodywork. The vehicle was tatty and probably wouldn't get through its next MOT, but otherwise there was nothing unusual or suspicious about it.

But the mere fact of the car's presence at least confirmed part of Simon's story. Feeling slightly more hopeful, Jardine approached the front door of the cottage and rapped on it with the heavy, old-fashioned knocker.

It was some time before Betty Duncan answered. She

half-opened the door, peering out at Jardine suspiciously.

It seemed a natural enough reaction, Jardine thought. The woman was in her sixties, the cottage was isolated, so a sense of caution was probably a sensible thing. He produced his ID card and waved it under Betty Duncan's nose.

'Sorry to bother you. DS Jardine, Maryhill Police Station. Are you the owner of the Fiat Panda parked outside?'

Betty eyed him warily. 'Yes,' she admitted.

'Did you happen to arrive home at around 4.30 this afternoon?'

Betty thought for a while, finally nodding. 'It would have been about that time, yes.'

Jardine cleared his throat, feeling a little embarrassed. The next question seemed ridiculous, but he had to ask it.

'Do you by any chance own a blue rain cape with a hood, and were you wearing it when you came home?'

Betty looked a little confused. 'I have a dark green raincoat,' she said. 'I think I was wearing it over my shoulders. Why? What's all this about?'

Jardine shuffled his feet awkwardly. 'Just a routine inquiry,' he muttered. 'Do you mind showing me the coat?'

Betty shrugged, as though humouring a madman. 'I'll just go and get it,' she said. 'You wait there.'

She disappeared inside the cottage for a few moments, eventually returning with a dark green raincoat over her arm. A cursory glance was enough for Jardine. He was already starting to back away from the door. 'That's fine, thank you. I'm sorry to have bothered you.'

Betty opened the door wider as he began to move away, stepping outside the cottage. 'Did I go through a red traffic light or something? My eyes aren't as good as they used to be.'

Jardine turned, smiling at her. 'No, it was someone else,' he said.

McVitie played the tape of Barrow's final message over for

the eighth time. He switched the recorder off and looked up at Taggart. '"Tell them to check . . ." Tell who?'

'I assume he meant for Elsa Chalmers to tell us, sir,' Taggart answered. 'I think he was suggesting that we should check other missing persons, not just Phillip Chalmers.'

McVitie looked pained. 'Good God, Jim. There must be hundreds.'

'Aye,' Taggart agreed with him. 'But we could try to narrow it down a bit, sir. Perhaps concentrate on men who have disappeared under similar circumstances — say just over the last year or two.'

McVitie nodded. It seemed to make sense. 'Any ideas at all on the "Gingerbread Men"?'

Taggart shook his head. 'Nothing, sir. Your guess would be as good as mine.' He stood up, pushing back his chair. 'Can I put a couple of people on checking back over our missing persons files, then?'

'Yes, of course,' McVitie said. His face suddenly took on a slightly sheepish, apologetic look. 'It looks as though you were right about there being a connection between Barrow's murder and the Chalmers case.'

Taggart allowed himself the satisfaction of a grin. 'I never doubted it for a second, sir,' he said wickedly.

Jardine was just coming in as he returned to his office. 'Have a nice afternoon in the woods?' Taggart asked him.

Jardine gave him a black look. 'I checked out Simon's latest "sighting". A sixty-year-old woman with a green rain-coat.'

'Oh, good,' Taggart said, still in an unusually jovial mood following McVitie's equally unusual apology. 'Glad you didn't waste your time, then.'

Chapter Nine

Jardine sometimes despaired of modern social workers. They seemed to live in the rarefied atmosphere of another planet for much of the time, taking and making arbitrary decisions about people's lives based on little more than some woolly theory absorbed during an Open University course.

The morning's proceedings — a case conference on the future of Simon and Nicola — had been a case in point.

His sense of depression showed on his face as he walked into the office.

'Did it not go too well?' Jackie Reid asked sympathetically.

Jardine scowled. 'The most important people involved weren't invited, of course. Simon and Nicola.'

Jackie knew the form. She'd been through it herself, several times. 'Of course not. It's only their future you're supposed to be deciding upon.'

'Anyway, the child psychologist seems to think that Simon is basically all right,' Jardine continued. 'He appears to be coping with the trauma of seeing his father murdered by playing detective. He also appears to have cast me in the role of father surrogate.'

Jackie opened her mouth to make a sarcastic comment, but thought better of it. She could see that Jardine wasn't in the mood for flippant remarks.

Any further conversation was pre-empted by Taggart, who chose that moment to throw open his door and bellow across the office.

'Jackie! Have you got that information for me yet?'

She scooped up a few sheets of paper from her desk. 'Coming, sir.'

Jardine followed her into Taggart's office. Jackie laid the papers down on his desk and gave him a few moments to scan through them.

'I've found three missing person cases which all bear a striking similarity to the Chalmers case,' she said finally. 'In all three cases, the victims were men. They all left home apparently on short visits — business trips, going shopping, a night out with the boys — that sort of thing. Each one of them disappeared without trace — and in each case their cars were subsequently found abandoned within half a mile of Central Station, just as Chalmers' was.'

Jardine had listened with interest and couldn't help putting in his own comment. 'Why has this pattern never shown up before?'

'This is over a period of two and a half years,' Jackie pointed out.

'And we've had more things to worry about than a few guys who wanted to take off,' Taggart added.

It was a valid point, Jardine conceded. The similarities wouldn't really have shown up unless one was specifically looking for a connection. 'What about Chalmers' wife?' he asked Taggart. 'Are you satisfied with her?'

Taggart glared at him. 'As a matter of fact I'm very dissatisfied,' he growled. 'I shall be having further words with that particular lady.'

Jackie reached down and picked up her report sheets. 'Shall I get on to checking these out then, sir?'

Taggart nodded. 'Aye, follow them all up. See if you can identify anything else these guys had in common.'

Jackie walked towards the door, holding it open for Jardine, expecting him to follow her. He didn't. Instead, he hovered in Taggart's office, fidgeting slightly.

'Well?' Taggart said, looking up.

'A personal matter, sir,' Jardine muttered. 'Something I wanted to ask you.'

Taggart looked peeved. 'So ask,' he said.

Jardine backed to the office door and closed it. 'It's about Gemma Normanton, sir — the writer. You saw her book the other day . . . *Flickering Candles.*'

'Ah, yes, the young lady who invites coppers out for dinner. Well, what about her?'

'The thing is, sir — she's currently researching a new book all about famous Glasgow murder cases,' Jardine carried on. 'And she would be very keen to talk to you about some of them — particularly the Balfour case and the Bowman and Samson killings.'

A look of incredulity spread across Taggart's face. 'Does she think that's all we have time for?' he asked.

Jardine shuffled his feet awkwardly. 'Well, anyway, I said I'd ask you,' he muttered lamely.

'And now you've asked,' Taggart snapped. 'And you know my answer.'

Jardine was obviously dismissed. He walked to the door and opened it, turning back briefly to Taggart. 'Thanks,' he said.

Taggart looked mystified. 'Thanks? Thanks for what?'

'For considering it,' Jardine said sarcastically. 'You could have just rejected the idea out of hand.'

He made a hasty exit.

Unaware that his future was being discussed that morning,

71

Simon continued to take the present very much under his own control. He had sneaked out of the house shortly after breakfast, cycled to Dunleath Woods and taken up a hiding place behind some blackberry bushes from where he could spy on Betty Duncan's cottage. Now, some four hours later, he was tired and hungry but, like a good detective, continued his vigil.

His patience was at last rewarded by the sight of the back door opening. Betty Duncan stepped out into the yard, took something from the old wooden shed and walked off into the woods.

It was the chance Simon had been waiting for. Crawling out from his hiding place, he loped across to the cottage, took one careful look about and sneaked in through the open back door.

Simon panned around the kitchen, his eyes taking everything in even though he was not sure what he was looking for. A large, barred game larder looked as though it might hide something interesting, but a quick tug on the handle told him that it was securely locked. There was a large, open pan steaming on top of the Aga cooker, in which something popped and bubbled thickly. Simon crossed to it, sniffing at something which he knew he should recognise but didn't.

It was toffee, he finally realised. The sweet smell reminded him of his hunger. For a moment the detective was forgotten and the hungry little boy took over. Simon wiped his finger around the outside edge of the pan, where some of the cooking toffee had boiled over and cooled down. He transferred the sticky finger to his mouth, sucking on it.

A sound behind him made him whirl round suddenly, and his stomach turned cold. Betty Duncan stood there framed in the doorway, a large axe raised menacingly in the air above her head. As Simon regarded her with horror, Betty stepped over the threshold and began to advance towards him.

Simon reacted in terror, pivoting on his heel and running round the large farmhouse table as Betty moved in his direction. More by luck than judgment, he was fortunate enough to wrong-foot her, so that she was caught halfway round the other side of the table as he started to run. Given a clear break to the open door, Simon dived out through it and began to run for his life through the woods to where he had hidden his bicycle.

'Oh, no you don't,' a gruff voice said suddenly. Simon found himself pinned tight in the vice-like grip of two thick, muscular arms. He struggled furiously for a few seconds, but there was no escape.

His captor turned him round by the shoulders. Simon found himself staring up at a veritable giant of a man clad in a checked work-shirt. On the forest floor, by his feet, lay a large industrial chainsaw and a pile of logs. The man glared down at Simon, his face grim and accusatory.

'I saw you running out of Betty's cottage. Been doing a bit of thieving, have you? Well, we'll soon see about that.'

The man began to march Simon back towards the cottage, despite the boy's frenzied protests.

Betty Duncan stepped out to meet them. She had laid the axe down by the door, and the expression on her face was one of curiosity more than anger.

'I caught him running away from your back door,' Joe Soutar told her. 'Looked like he'd been up to no good.'

'I didn't steal anything,' Simon said, protesting his innocence.

Soutar did not seem convinced. He marched Simon into the kitchen and sat him down at the table. 'So, what were you doing, sneaking around in somebody else's home?'

'I was hungry. I smelled the toffee cooking,' Simon said, hoping that the partial truth would be sufficient.

'Don't they feed you at home, then?' Soutar demanded — but he sounded a little more understanding.

Betty Duncan had walked across the kitchen as Soutar had dragged Simon in. Now she returned with a huge fruit-cake and two plates. She cut two large slices of cake and placed them on the table.

'Leave him be, Joe. He's only a boy,' she said. 'Besides, I

probably gave him the fright of his life. I'd been out chopping firewood and I had the axe in my hand when I came back to the cottage and found him.'

She looked down at Simon, her haggard old face creasing into a smile. 'Do your parents know you're running around in these woods on your own?'

Simon averted his eyes from hers. 'My parents are never at home,' he muttered quietly.

'Well, that's still no excuse for breaking into people's houses,' Soutar put in, still suspicious. He finished his slab of cake and stood up. 'I'd better be getting back to work. Will you be all right with him, Betty?'

Betty Duncan nodded. 'Thank you, Joe. We'll both be just fine now. It's a long time since I had a boy come to tea.'

Soutar pushed his huge frame up from the table and sauntered towards the door.

Relaxing slightly, Simon picked up his piece of cake and began to eat it hungrily.

'Would you like a nice cup of tea?' Betty asked.

Simon nodded wordlessly. Betty crossed to the Aga, lifted off the old brass kettle and made a fresh pot. Pouring a steaming mug, she carried it back to Simon and sat down, regarding him almost fondly.

'Yes, it's been a long, long time since I had children in the house,' she murmured distantly. 'My children are all grown up now, and they never come back to see me.' She pushed another slice of cake across the table to Simon. 'Are you an only child?'

'I've got a sister. She's five,' Simon told her.

'And where is she?' Betty wanted to know.

'At home.'

'Without your parents?'

The mixture of half-lies, half-truths was getting complicated. 'Sometimes they're home, sometimes they're not,' Simon said hurriedly. 'Today they're home.'

'And that's where you should be,' Betty said, suddenly glancing up at the old cuckoo clock which hung on the wall.

'It'll be getting dark in an hour or so. You'd best be off as soon as you've finished your tea.'

She suddenly seemed very anxious to get rid of him, Simon felt. Now that it seemed clear that the old woman posed no obvious threat, he had realised that he hadn't really learned anything.

'I could come and see you again,' he suggested.

Betty Duncan looked enthusiastic at the prospect. 'You could bring your little sister. I'll make a special children's tea for you both.'

She walked across to the kitchen dresser and took out a pen and a slip of paper. 'I'll write my number down for you,' she said, scribbling on the paper. She handed it to Simon. 'But you must promise to ring me first, to tell me when you're coming.'

Simon took the paper, folded it and slipped it into his pocket. He drained his mug of tea and crammed the last piece of cake into his mouth.

Betty walked with him to the front door of the cottage and waved him on his way. 'Remember, you must always call to say you're coming,' she called after him. 'You must *never* come without ringing. Do you understand?'

Simon waved back to her, nodding his head and taking the message to heart. For some odd reason that he didn't quite understand, it seemed particularly important to the old woman.

He walked slowly back towards his bike, deep in thought. There was something very odd about Betty Duncan he had decided.

Elsa Chalmers did not seem particularly surprised to see Taggart standing on her doorstep again. It was almost as if she had been expecting him.

'I hope you don't mind me calling by,' Taggart said. 'Just a few more questions I wanted to ask you.'

A wry smile played over Elsa's attractive mouth. 'I'd hardly say that driving from Glasgow to Edinburgh falls into the category of "passing by" — but you'd better come in any-way.' Graciously, she showed him into the house and invited him to sit down in the lounge. 'Can I get you a cup of tea or something?'

Taggart shook his head. 'No, this really is a fleeting call. It's just that the last time I spoke to you, I think I might have got the wrong impression.'

Elsa lifted one eyebrow fractionally. 'Oh, really? And what impression was that?'

'The impression that you didn't really care whether your husband came back or not,' Taggart said bluntly.

He had expected the woman to show some degree of of-fence, but her face was a bland, impenetrable mask. 'That's absolute nonsense,' she said firmly.

Taggart regarded her curiously. 'Is it, I wonder?' he mused. 'I'd like to think that if I went missing, and my wife went to the trouble and expense of hiring a private detective, she'd at least stay around to see what he turned up.'

Still Elsa refused to be drawn out. 'I'd imagine that was up the the individual woman,' she observed. 'Different women behave in different ways.'

'Oh, of course,' Taggart agreed. 'But I'm sure that if my wife really needed to go off on holiday she'd make arrange-ments for the private detective to stay in touch.'

'Which is exactly what I did,' Elsa pointed out.

Taggart shook his head. 'No, Mrs Chalmers. You left only an emergency system for if something important turned up. But what about the unimportant day-to-day things? Were they just to wait until you got back?'

'A clumsy expression, perhaps,' Elsa said, starting to be-come more defensive.

Taggart felt encouraged by this response. Assuming that he had her on the run, he stepped up the pressure.

'Mrs Chalmers, I'm investigating a particularly brutal murder which seems to involve the disappearance of your husband,' he went on in a much more aggressive tone. 'Now, you can either tell me the whole truth here, or I can arrange

76

for it to be in an interview room in a Glasgow police station.'

It was not a prospect Elsa Chalmers relished. Just as Taggart had expected, she caved in immediately. She sighed deeply. 'All right. You're obviously going to be persistent.' She paused for a couple of seconds. 'The plain fact of the matter is that I need Phillip back so that I can divorce him.'

'Or you need proof that he's dead,' Taggart put in.

Elsa shrugged, conceding the point. She stood up, starting to pace up and down the room. 'Do you know how difficult it is to get a divorce from a husband who is just missing?' she asked. 'Not technically presumed dead for seven years? Oh, you can go to court, perhaps bring things forward — but it's still a very long wait, and in all that time everything is frozen. Our bank account, this house, all the assets. The law says I can't dispose of anything for a very long time.'

She turned away, looking out through the window. Taggart leaned forward in his chair and picked something out of the ashtray on the nearby coffee-table.

'Did Phillip know you wanted a divorce?'

Elsa turned round. 'Yes,' she said simply.

'And did he intend making it easy?'

'Not exactly. He said he still loved me.'

Taggart held up the object from the ashtray between his finger and thumb. It was a bright blue cigarette stub with a gold tip. 'Where is he, Mrs Chalmers?' he muttered softly.

Bobby Gault stepped into the lounge from the conservatory. 'Well, I assume you've more or less put it all together?' he said smoothly.

'More or less. But why don't you spell it our for me anyway?'

'Elsa asked Phillip for a divorce to marry me. He refused,' Gault said. 'A few days later he disappears and his car is found abandoned in Glasgow. How do you think it might have looked?'

'As though you two had plotted to kill him,' Taggart said.

'Quite,' Gault murmured, as though that explained and excused everything.

Taggart was quietly fuming. 'Why didn't you tell me all this two days ago?' he demanded.

Gault gave him a thin, knowing smile. 'Come on, Taggart. We both know how our colleagues' minds work.'

'But we're in the same job, for God's sake,' Taggart protested.

'But not in the same force,' Gault pointed out. 'I didn't know how much I could trust you.'

Taggart bristled at the implication. 'Right now I wouldn't trust the pair of you with the pennies on a dead man's eyes,' he muttered savagely.

Elsa could see that it was getting personal, a male challenge thing. She stepped in to mediate. 'Look, it must make a difference now that other missing person cases are involved. It isn't just Phillip anymore.'

'The only person who says so is the private detective who *you* hired,' Taggart snapped, turning on her. 'And now he's dead — murdered.' He paused for effect, glaring at each of them in turn. 'Which, from where I'm standing, make you both look in a very sticky position indeed,' he added finally.

Chapter Ten

Jackie Reid hadn't directly asked Jardine for his help but he had offered it anyway, sensing that she would probably appreciate a bit of back-up even though it was not strictly necessary.

It was not an easy or pleasant job, going back to missing person cases after such a long period — especially when there was no new information, or even a crumb of comfort, to offer the victims' families. But the mere fact of opening up old wounds again was bound to cause upset, and renewed police interest almost certain to raise false hopes again. All in all, Jardine had felt more than justified in taking a couple of hours off from other duties to accompany Jackie on her interviews.

They had been told that they would find Cathy Ross in the park, by the children's playground.

'Refresh my memory,' Jardine said quietly as they walked across the grass towards the play area.

'Archie Ross, aged thirty-four,' Jackie said, without needing to refer to her case notes. 'Disappeared fourteen months ago on a simple shopping trip one late Friday afternoon. Family man, steady job, no police record. On the face of it, a solid citizen — although a couple of his male friends suggested that he'd been a bit of a lad before marrying his pregnant girlfriend and felt a bit trapped by the responsibilities of parenthood.'

They had reached the playground. A woman fitting Cathy's description was sitting alone on a park bench, watching a three-year-old boy playing on the roundabout.

Jardine and Jackie approached her.

'Mrs Ross?' Jardine asked softly. The woman looked up, nodding. Jardine produced his ID card. 'Detective Sergeant Jardine, Maryhill Police Station. This is DC Jackie Reid. We've come to ask you a few questions about your husband's disappearance.'

Cathy's initial look of surprise was replaced by one of hope. Her eyes lit up. It was the reaction Jardine had expected, and secretly dreaded.

'Look, I must point out that we don't have any real new information or hopes to offer you,' he added quickly. 'Just a potential new line of inquiry.'

Cathy's face fell. 'Then why are you here?'

Jackie Reid sat down on the bench beside her. 'I'm sorry, Mrs Ross, but we need to go over the facts of your husband's disappearance with you again,' she murmured in a gentle, sympathetic tone. 'Could you just tell us exactly what happened on the last afternoon you saw him?'

Cathy sighed deeply, her bottom lip trembling slightly as she spoke. 'He went out to buy a birthday present for our son. He never came back. He phoned from town to say that he couldn't find the game that Peter wanted, but he was going to carry on trying, look in a few more shops.'

'What time was this?' Jardine wanted to know.

'It was around six o'clock,' Cathy said. 'I remember, because I said I'd put his dinner in the oven for him. It was his favourite — steak and kidney pudding.'

'But surely, all the shops would be closed at that time,' Jackie pointed out.

Cathy Ross shook her head. 'It was a Thursday. There's late-night shopping on a Thursday. That's why I didn't get too worried until it was very late. I thought he might have met one of his friends and decided to have a snack in a pub or something.'

'Did he do that often?' Jardine asked. 'Go off to the pub with his mates?'

Cathy looked up at him with defiance blazing in her eyes. 'That was what you people suggested last time,' she said, with more than a trace of bitterness in her voice. 'Said that he probably didn't want the responsibility of a family, or had another woman somewhere. But he wasn't like that. I knew — he just wasn't like that. He wouldn't have run off and left us.'

Her son came running across from the playground. Cathy stood up, scooping him into her arms and hugging him protectively against her.

'Peter, this lady and gentleman are police officers,' she told him. 'They've come to ask about Daddy.' She paused, glaring into Jardine's eyes. 'A year too late,' she added bitterly.

Setting the boy down, she grasped his hand and began to walk away. Jardine and Jackie fell into step beside her.

'When you got your husband's car back, did you notice anything unusual about the interior?' Jackie asked.

'Such as?'

'Were there any crumbs on the driver's seat, for instance?'

Cathy stopped dead in her tracks. She regarded Jackie with bemusement. 'After all this time, you expect me to remember that?'

'Does "Gingerbread Men" mean anything to you?' Jardine put in.

Cathy whirled on him, confused and angry. 'Look, why has it taken you all this time to even show an interest? Archie's been gone for over a year. Peter's had no father for all that time . . . and now all you can do is to come round stirring everything up again and asking damn stupid questions.'

Jardine attempted to pacify her. 'I'm sorry, Mrs Ross — but there really is a good reason for the questions, please believe me,' he said gently.

But Cathy was already beyond pacifying. 'Do you know where he is?' she demanded. 'Do you even *think* you know where he is?'

Jardine shook his head sadly. 'No, I'm sorry. We don't,' he admitted.

'Then, please, leave us alone,' Cathy said quietly, her voice breaking on a sob. 'Just go away and leave us alone.'

She began to walk away again. 'It's funny, isn't it?' she observed. 'When a woman goes missing suddenly, all the stops get pulled out. But when it's a man, you couldn't care less.'

Jardine and Jackie let her go. Jardine watched her walk away with her son.

'You know, that's not strictly true,' he muttered to Jackie, almost defensively.

Jackie smiled ruefully. 'It is from where she's standing,' she said flatly.

Jardine pulled up outside a modest, but smart-looking semi-detached house in a quiet and upper-price-range suburb. He glanced sideways at Jackie as she flipped through her notes.

'What's the score on this one?'

'Frank Innes, aged sixty-five at the time of his disappearance,' Jackie said. 'The oldest case which fits the pattern, and possibly the most baffling. An elderly man, retired with a more than adequate company pension and no pressures, no worries. Not at all the sort of person you might expect to do a moonlight.'

Mrs Innes seemed far more relaxed and philosophical about things than Cathy Ross. But then, after two and a half years she had probably become resigned to the facts, Jardine thought. After explaining the reason for their visit, Jardine and Jackie were shown into a well-furnished lounge and given a cup of tea. The woman seemed almost chirpy.

'I don't get many visitors these days,' she explained, smiling at them warmly. She sipped her tea, regarding them both with vague curiosity. 'So, you want me to tell you about Frank's disappearance again.'

'If you don't mind, Mrs Innes,' Jackie said quietly.

The woman smiled wistfully. 'It's funny, isn't it? I still call it "Frank's disappearance". I suppose I always found it easier to cope with that way. Well, what can I tell you?'

'Tell us how your husband was prior to his disappearance,' Jardine suggested. 'Was he upset in any way, did he have any worries on his mind, that sort of thing.'

Mrs Innes thought carefully, finally shaking her grey head. 'There was nothing,' she said. 'It was just an ordinary day, really.' She paused for a moment. 'Of course, Frank hadn't been his usual cheery self for some time. He'd had a stroke about six months previously and it changed his personality. Strokes can do that, the doctor told me. It made him more restless, easily aggravated. But we'd learned to cope, as we'd always done. We'd been married for forty-six years, after all.'

'And he just went shopping?' Jackie put in, cutting her short.

Mrs Innes nodded. 'All the shopping was still in the boot of the car when they found it. Bread, fresh vegetables, steak from the butcher's. Frank liked his bit of steak. I went round to all the shops afterwards, asking them questions. He'd seemed perfectly normal. Then he phoned me to tell me that he'd bought everything, and that he loved me very much, and that he'd be home soon.'

Mrs Innes broke off suddenly, her composure cracking a little. Jardine saw tears pricking out in her eyes. He pulled a clean handkerchief from his pocket, handing it to her.

Mrs Innes dabbed at her eyes, struggling to control herself again.

'That was the really strange thing,' she continued after a while. 'In all the years we had been married, he had never phoned me to tell me that he loved me before.'

'Was it a happy marriage?' Jardine asked.

The woman smiled again, remembering a lifetime of good moments. 'Blissful,' she said emphatically. 'Heavenly. We never had any problems that we couldn't sort out together. You can ask anyone — ask our children.'

Her face clouded over. 'But even if he was going to leave me, why would he do all the shopping first?'

'It certainly doesn't seem very logical,' Jackie admitted, agreeing with her.

'And that's exactly what I said to the police at the time. Not logical. And then to leave the car in a side street like that. I mean, if you're going to disappear, why not drive it away to wherever you're going?'

'Mrs Innes — does "Gingerbread Men" mean anything to you?' Jardine asked.

The woman looked baffled. 'Gingerbread Men? I'm afraid I don't understand.'

'Neither do we, really,' Jackie admitted. She placed her cup and saucer down on the coffee-table and started to rise to her feet.

'Frank liked his cakes,' Mrs Innes was saying. 'He had a really sweet tooth.'

Jardine caught the warning look which Jackie was flashing in his direction and got the message. Sad as it was, they really didn't have time to sit around and keep a lonely old woman company while she reminisced about her departed husband. He followed Jackie's lead, rising to his feet.

'What do *you* think happened to your husband, Mrs Innes?' he asked as a parting shot.

The woman was in no doubt. 'I think he's dead,' she said with an air of finality. 'I don't know why, but I think he committed suicide, and that's why he telephoned me to say that he loved me. He'd never done that before, you see.'

There was really nothing to add after that. Neither Jardine

nor Jackie saw much point in offering the woman even a slim ray of hope. As she had said, she had accepted her husband's death and learned to cope with it.

They made their way to the front door. Mrs Innes showed them out, smiling after them. They walked slowly down the path as the door closed behind them.

'What else have we got?' Jardine asked.

Jackie consulted her notes. 'There's another one in Edinburgh, but we can leave it until tomorrow. Ian Scott, nineteen. Came to Glasgow on 5 July last year to go to the Citizens' Theatre. Phoned his mother after the play to say that he was going to a nightclub with some friends, and that was the last time she heard from him. Car found a few days later, just like the others.'

They had reached the car. Jackie stopped, looking up at Jardine. 'None of the victims seem to have any relationship to the others, do they?'

Jardine regarded her thoughtfully, a thin smile on his lips. 'There is one thing in common,' he corrected her. 'The ET factor.'

Jackie gave him a puzzled look. 'The ET factor?' She didn't understand.

'Haven't you noticed? So far, every single one of them phoned home before disappearing,' Jardine said, spelling it out for her.

Chapter Eleven

Jimmy Buchanan pulled his car to a halt beside the empty telephone-box, checking his watch. It was just after half-past six. Time to call his wife and tell her he wouldn't be coming home after all. She would understand, or he hoped she would — especially when he told her the good news. The wife of a travelling salesman had to get used to her husband spending nights away from home.

He climbed out of the car and stepped into the phone-box. Dialling his home number, he waited for his wife to answer.

'Hello, love, it's me. Just thought I'd ring to tell you the good news. I had a meeting this afternoon with Mr Panasoutis, and he's agreed to extend my territory, like I wanted.'

Jimmy paused, sighing, as his wife went into a minor tirade. As he had half-expected, she had seized upon the single negative aspect of his new promotion.

'Well, of course it's good news,' he protested finally, when he could get a word in edgeways. 'I'll be bringing home a much fatter commission cheque each month, for a start. And as for having to spend more days away from home, we'll just have to get used to it.'

The point brought him to the main reason for his phone call. He took a breath before speaking again. 'As a matter of fact, I'm going to have to stay away tonight. I have an appointment with a big buyer first thing in the morning. Could be worth a regular three or four hundred a month.'

Jimmy paused again while his wife launched into her usual list of objections. Most of them concerned his welfare, he had to admit. In a slightly resigned tone, he answered them all in turn.

'Yes, of course I'll get a proper meal. Yes, I will stay in a decent hotel and yes, I can claim it on expenses. Now don't worry about me, I'll be fine. I'll have something to eat and then go to a bingo hall or something. I feel lucky tonight.'

His wife appeared to be mollified. Jimmy listened to her protestation of love and devotion with a wry smile on his face.

'Of course I love you too,' he said finally. 'And I'll be home tomorrow afternoon. We'll go out for dinner tomorrow night, to celebrate. I'll take you to that new Indian place — you know, the one which looks like the Taj Majal from the outside.'

With a slightly embarrassed glance out of the side of the phone-box, Jimmy blew a kiss down the phone and replaced the receiver. Grinning broadly he opened the phone-box door and looked around the Glasgow streets with an air of optimistic expectancy. It had been quite some time since he had enjoyed a real night out on the town.

Returning to his car, Jimmy started it up and headed for the seamier side of the city. There was a particular bingo hall one of his customers had told him about. A lively, boisterous place with a drag queen caller who cracked outrageously blue jokes. It sounded fun. It would do for a start, anyway.

In fact, the place turned out to be somewhat less than it had been cracked up to be. It was all rather shabby, even sordid, Jimmy concluded — and the somewhat down-market Julian Clary impersonator's jokes were restricted to old and weary one-liners aimed at the predominantly female clientele. But he had bought a ten-game card at the door and it seemed point-less to waste it by walking out. Jimmy had found himself a stool next to a rather pretty blonde-haired girl and her older female companion, and sat down to play. He was now on his seventh game and was starting to feel a bit fed-up.

'Sixty-nine,' the drag queen was calling out in a high-pitched, camp voice. 'Or *soixante-neuf*, if you speak French like I do.' He fluttered his false eyelashes at a bunch of women in the front row. 'Didn't know I was bi, did you girls? Bi-lingual, that is.' He waggled his tongue in and out of his mouth in an overtly obscene gesture. 'Got the gift of tongue, if you know what I mean.'

Jimmy found it all rather distasteful and embarrassing. He glanced sideways, wondering how the girls beside him were taking it.

The blonde merely looked bored, but strangely innocent, as if the crudity was going over her head. Her companion's face was almost totally hidden by her long black hair, but her eyes were dead-looking and her mouth pulled into a hard, almost contemptuous sneer. She was at least fifteen years older than the blonde girl, Jimmy realised. He wondered briefly what their relationship was. They seemed an oddly mismatched pair.

As he looked at them the young girl turned towards him slightly and their eyes met. Jimmy smiled shyly, slightly embar-rassed to have been caught staring at her, but the blonde didn't seem to mind. She smiled back briefly, then returned her eyes to her bingo card.

Jimmy concentrated on his own game again, noting with a

slight shock of excitement that he only had one number to go for a full house.

'Twenty-one,' the caller announced, and started to make some crack about virgins.

But Jimmy wasn't listening. Having ticked off his last number, he was on his feet waving his hands and shouting excitedly. 'House! I've got a house.'

Triumphantly, he held his winning ticket aloft and started to push through the people seated beside him. Briefly he glanced down at the blonde girl, his eyes bright. 'I knew I was feeling lucky tonight,' he announced with a grin.

The girl's face registered a smile in return, but it was little more than a brief cosmetic mask over a tired, world-weary expression which seemed to belie her tender years.

The bar was a rough and ready sort of place, but lively and friendly enough. Eager to celebrate his £150 win, Jimmy had picked the first pub he had found after leaving the bingo hall, and had already consumed three or four pints when he saw the blonde girl and her companion walk into the place. They made their way to the bar and propped themselves up on two stools.

Emboldened by drink, Jimmy got up from his table and moved towards the bar, edging in beside the blonde.

'Hello again,' he said, smiling. 'I was sitting next to you in the bingo hall, remember? Look, can I buy you a drink?'

The girl looked at him without any real enthusiasm. 'I'll have a half of lager — and a vodka for my friend,' she said in a lilting Irish brogue.

Jimmy ordered the drinks from the barman and turned back to the girl. 'It's a bit lonely, celebrating on your own.'

She managed a faint half-smile. 'Oh, we wouldn't want you to be that.'

'What part of Ireland are you from?' Jimmy asked, forcing a conversation.

'County Clare.'

Jimmy nodded knowingly. 'Lovely part of the country. I went there once, on a caravanning holiday. Great people, the Irish. I'm Jimmy, by the way.'

'I'm Jenny,' the girl said. She jerked her head towards her dark-haired companion. 'That's Ann.'

The older woman made no attempt to communicate, or even smile. She continued to stare morosely over the bar, taking up her vodka when it was served and draining it at a single gulp.

Jimmy was thinking about offering her another when the drag queen from the bingo hall strode up to the bar, wrapping his arms around the shoulders of the two girls.

'Hi, girls. Losers tonight, are we? Still, at least you're chatting up the winners.'

Ann spoke for the first time. 'I'm a bloody loser every sodding night,' she complained miserably.

'No customer tonight?' the drag queen asked.

Ann glanced sideways at Jenny. 'She has.'

Jimmy hadn't quite fallen in to what was going on around him. 'Customer?' he echoed blankly.

Jenny looked at him, hastily changing the subject. 'So what do you do for a living, Jimmy?'

'I'm a rep for a confectionery company. Travelling salesman, you know.'

Ann looked sideways down the bar, a sneering look on her face. 'Are you giving out free samples?' she demanded.

Jimmy was a little taken aback. 'No,' he muttered uncertainly.

'Well, neither is she,' Ann snapped. 'We're working girls, dearie — on the game. Get it?'

Jimmy felt rather naïve and foolish. The thought hadn't crossed his mind. He struggled for something to say to cover his embarrassment.

'Oh, well, we all have to do something for a living,' he managed, rather weakly. He looked at Jenny more closely. She was even younger than he had first supposed — eighteen at most. 'You look too nice,' he muttered lamely.

Gavin, the drag queen, made a camp little gesture with his hands. 'Ooh, you hear all the original chat-up lines in here, don't you?'

Jimmy ignored him. 'Look, I've got my car outside,' he said to Jenny. 'We could go for a drive, if you fancy it.'

The girl looked slightly suspicious. 'Drive where?'

Jimmy looked sheepish again. 'I don't know, really. I don't know Glasgow very well. I thought you might have somewhere . . . you know, where you take people.'

It was the girl's turn to look slightly embarrassed. 'I haven't been doing this for very long,' she said.

Jimmy found himself feeling sorry for her. She was like a little girl lost in a big and frightening city. 'Look, let's take a drive, anyway,' he suggested kindly. 'We can just sit and talk, if you like. I've got plenty of money — I won a hundred and fifty pounds at the bingo.'

'Okay.' Jenny made up her mind quickly. She drained her half of lager and stood up, ready to follow Jimmy out to the car.

Behind them Ann fished surreptitiously in her handbag and drew out a small note-pad and ballpoint pen. As they started to walk out, she followed them at a discreet distance.

She paused in the pub doorway, keeping out of sight as Jimmy led the way to his parked car and opened the door for Jenny like a true gentleman. As they climbed in, Ann wrote down the car number-plate registration on her pad and slipped it back into her bag.

She glanced sideways at Gavin, who had followed her out. 'You can't be too careful these days,' she observed as Jimmy's car drove away.

She watched the car until it was out of sight and then turned and went back into the bar.

Chapter Twelve

Jardine paused uncertainly outside the regular police pub with Gemma on his arm. He was torn between an egotistical male desire to show her off to his colleagues and the fear that Taggart, or Jackie Reid, would say or do something to embarrass him.

Male ego, and Gemma's insistence that he contrive a meeting with Taggart, won the day. Pushing open the door, he ushered Gemma into the crowded pub and made his way to the bar where Taggart, McVitie and Dr Andrews were all clustered together like the three witches from *Macbeth*.

Jardine pushed Gemma in front of him like a trophy. 'Sir, I'd like you to meet Gemma Normanton, the crime writer,' he said to Taggart.

Taggart was caught on the hop. He cast a quick and baleful glare at Jardine before switching on a smile and turning to the girl. He opened his mouth to say something pleasant, but never got the chance to put it into words.

'Good heavens, yes. You're the young lady who has just

published that book on prisoners on America's Death Row,' Dr Andrews exclaimed. 'I haven't read it myself yet, but I'm told it's an excellent book. I'm very pleased to meet you.'

Andrews held out his hand, which Gemma accepted and shook warmly.

Taggart was left with his mouth open, gaping like a fish out of water. Hastily, he returned to his pint on the counter.

'The research for that must have been fascinating,' McVitie said, introducing himself.

Gemma nodded. 'But harrowing. I found that I quite got to like some of them. In fact, a couple of prisoners still write to me.'

'I can believe it,' McVitie said with a knowing nod. 'So, tell me, what are you working on now?'

'A book on famous Glasgow murder cases,' Gemma told him.

'Well, you've certainly come to the right place,' Andrews put in. 'I could tell you some really interesting forensic details — going right back to the Gallagher acid-bath killings in the early 1950s.'

'Actually, Gemma's more interested in some of our more recent cases,' Jardine interrupted, cutting him short. 'Including those that Mr Taggart and I worked on together.'

It was a crude ploy to get Taggart into the conversation, but it failed to work. Andrews and McVitie were like flies round a jampot.

'Of course, I've been in overall charge of all murder cases for the past twelve years,' McVitie announced proudly.

Gemma had no choice but to respond. 'Oh, really? Then I would be very interested to talk to you about a few of the more interesting cases — such as the Black Pudding Shop murder.'

'Ah, yes. That was an intriguing case,' Andrews said, bouncing back into the limelight. 'That was where they cut up the drug dealer and had us all crawling about in rubbish incinerators for days searching for the head.'

Taggart suddenly got to his feet, draining his glass with

unusual haste. His face was impassive, but Jardine could tell that he was inwardly fuming, his nose well and truly out of joint.

'Well, if you'll all excuse me, I think Jean has a cup of cocoa waiting for me in the microwave,' he announced curtly. He nodded briefly at Gemma by way of farewell and stormed out of the pub. His departure hardly caused a ripple, McVitie and Dr Andrews continuing to vie for the attention of a beautiful woman young enough to be their daughter and Jardine struggling to get a word in edgeways.

He gave up, eventually, accepting the fact that he was, for the moment anyway, superfluous. Gemma seemed happy enough, he realised, cleverly pumping the two men for research information under cover of polite conversation. Jardine relaxed, taking comfort from the rare and wonderful experience of watching Andrews and McVitie actually fight for the privilege of buying rounds of drinks.

The rest of the evening slipped away until closing time, finally giving Jardine the chance to re-establish himself. He slipped his arm around Gemma's slim waist possessively.

'Well, I suppose we'd better be off.' It gave him a minor thrill of pleasure to see the pained look which crossed both men's faces.

Later, curled up on the sofa with Gemma across his lap and with some smoochy late-night music playing, Jardine recalled the look on Taggart's face, and grinned wickedly.

'I thought he was going to stamp his feet and throw a tantrum,' he murmured.

Gemma looked at him dreamily. 'Who?'

'Taggart,' Jardine said. 'I've never seen his nose so out of joint.'

'Well, I think he's a sweetie,' Gemma said.

Jardine looked down at her in surprise. 'I've heard him called some things, but never that before.' He snuggled down in the sofa, idly stroking Gemma's hair. 'Like the music?'

Gemma thought for a while. 'It's a bit romantic,' she observed. It sounded almost like a complaint.

Jardine regarded her curiously. 'What's so wrong with romance?'

Gemma smiled wistfully. 'Nothing, I suppose. I've just had a lot of it knocked out of me.'

Jardine hugged her. 'Can't you escape from that?' he murmured softly.

Gemma sat up suddenly, looking him directly in the eyes. There was a deeply serious, even slightly sad, expression on her face.

'Meeting people who are queuing up to die? You don't escape from an experience like that, Mike. The best you can do is to try and forget — for a while, at least.'

Jardine bent to kiss her. 'Then forget,' he whispered.

Gemma responded to the kiss for a few seconds, then pulled away again. 'Seriously, Mike — I want you to realise something,' she said. 'I'm not the dewy-eyed little girl you knew sixteen years ago. I've changed, Mike. I've changed a lot. I'm not sure that you'd like some of those changes.'

Jardine cuddled her reassuringly. 'I like you just fine,' he murmured softly, kissing her again.

This time Gemma did not pull away. The kiss lasted for a long time. Finally, Gemma stood up and reached down for Jardine's hand, pulling him to his feet. She glanced around the flat at her luggage and possessions. 'Come on, Mike — let's go to bed,' she said quietly. 'I can unpack in the morning.'

Jardine allowed her to pull him gently but insistently towards the bedroom. There seemed no point in telling her that he had prepared a bed in the spare room.

In Dunleath Woods the silence of the night was shattered by a single, short, but blood-curdling scream. Jimmy Buchanan's head thudded softly against a carpeted floor, his dead eyes staring sightlessly up at the ceiling. Blood streamed from his slashed throat down over his naked shoulders and chest.

He would not be home by early afternoon as he had promised his wife. He would not be home again, ever. Jimmy's lucky day had finally ended.

Betty Duncan's old eyes were heavy with sadness and more than a hint of fear. The nightmare was abroad again, the terror newly alive and sucking her into its bloody gaping maw once again.

She shuddered, fighting to control the conflict which threatened to tear her mind apart. There was work — important work — that had to be done. Betty knew that she had to pull herself together, prepare herself for the grisly task which fate had chosen for her. There was no one else. She had no choice.

Later, much later, she dragged Jimmy's body awkwardly through the cottage kitchen and out through the door into the back yard. She was calmer now, resigned to the unpleasant job and more comfortable with the familiar routine of it all.

Finally, it was done. Betty emptied the last of the petrol over Jimmy Buchanan's funeral pyre and tossed in a lighted match. Once again the dark forest was strangely illuminated by the roaring column of fire which belched from the top of the incinerator.

On the windowsill of the cottage Betty's black cat sat watching the proceedings with detached, feline disinterest. Only the radiated warmth from the fire gave it any pleasure. Purring softly, it basked lazily, its sleek black fur and green eyes reflecting the distorted shapes of the leaping flames.

Chapter Thirteen

Betty Duncan washed her hands under a running tap in the kitchen sink. Dark red stains merged into the running water, blending and diluting into lighter coloured rivulets which swirled around the white bowl and down the plughole.

There was a sudden loud rapping on the kitchen door. Betty looked up, startled. Hastily she dried her hands on a nearby towel and walked to the door, opening it.

The midday sunshine streamed into the cottage kitchen. Simon and Nicola stood on the step, hand in hand and looking up nervously at her.

Betty's face cracked into a smile. She bent down, placing her hands on Nicola's small shoulders. 'You must be Nicola,' she said in a gentle, kindly voice. 'Come in, both of you. Everything's almost ready.'

Nicola was shy and apprehensive, but with Simon prodding her insistently from behind she took a tentative step over the threshold. Betty ushered them into the cosy kitchen, her face beaming. 'Wait till you see what I've prepared for you,' she promised.

Simon and Nicola walked in, gaping at the kitchen table in utter astonishment as Betty proudly displayed her surprise treat. The table looked as though it had been set out for an entire army of children. Laden with cakes of all shapes and sizes, jellies, trifles and biscuits, it was a veritable banquet of sweetness. Yet there was something almost sinister about it as well, Simon couldn't help feeling. The sticky, sickly delights piled upon the table looked wildly overdone, almost too good to be true. For some strange reason Simon found himself thinking of bait on a trap.

'I was just going to make a nice blackberry pie as well,' Bett announced. 'But the time ran out. Never mind, I'll do one the next time you come.'

She crossed back to the sink, where a large colander full of blackberries stood. Taking a wet dishcloth, Betty wiped away the last of the red stains where the juice had run on to the white enamel, and tipped the washed fruit into a bowl. She wiped her hands on her pinafore and stared at the table, a worried frown crossing her face. There was something missing, something she had forgotten.

Her face brightened suddenly. 'Drinks, I forgot the drinks,' she said. She hurried across to a cupboard and drew out two large plastic bottles of lemonade, setting them down on the table. 'Now, come and sit down, the both of you,' she said indicating two chairs.

Nicola sat down warily, her natural shyness fighting excitement with the array of goodies displayed before her eyes. Betty placed a plate in front of her, selecting a particularly gooey and sickly-sweet cake for a starter.

'Now, eat up. Everything has to be eaten. Every single cake and biscuit,' Betty said, fussing round like an excited mother hen.

Simon took his seat, reviewing the laden table with suspicion. He couldn't get the strange feeling out of his head that there was something very wrong with the whole situation. He wondered, fancifully, if the food was poisoned.

Betty thrust a plate of trifle under his nose. 'Come on, Simon. Eat up. Don't make your little sister eat it all on her own.'

Simon glanced sideways at Nicola, who was now tucking into her sticky cake with relish. She appeared to be enjoying herself, he thought. But then she was younger, more innocent. She probably couldn't sense the strangeness that he could.

Almost reluctantly Simon picked up a spoon and began to eat his trifle, pleasantly surprised to find that it tasted very good indeed.

'Just one more thing,' Betty suddenly announced, remembering her final treat. She walked over to the Aga cooker, opening the oven door and pulling out a large flat baking-tray. She transferred the contents to a plate and carried it to the table.

'Gingerbread men,' Betty said. 'A party's not complete without gingerbread men.'

Simon regarded this latest addition to the table with trepidation. There were at least a dozen of the large, thick biscuits on the plate, each one decorated with currants for eyes and coat buttons. They alone would fill his belly twice over — yet Betty seemed insistent that everything on the table had to be consumed. He could only hope that she didn't get too upset when most of the food was left over, as it was bound to be.

Upset was not the word in the Frazer household. Simon's latest disappearing act had caused consternation for just about everybody. Willie Frazer looked at Jackie Reid apologetically.

'We just turned our backs for a moment, and he was gone. Only this time he's taken Nicola with him.'

'A regular little Houdini is our Simon,' Brockwell put in. Of all of them, he seemed least worried.

'I'm sure he won't let any harm come to Nicola,' Jackie said to Jessie Frazer, who was particularly upset. 'Remember, he did save her life once. I think he's pretty devoted to her.'

Jardine returned to the room from using the phone in the lobby.

'Well, Gemma says that he hasn't turned up at my place, so he could be anywhere.' He looked at Frazer with a faintly accusing expression on his face. 'Aren't you people given any special training to stop this sort of thing happening?'

Frazer faced him squarely. 'We are emergency foster parents. We take in other people's children at a moment's notice, and we do the best we can for them.'

'Often troubled children, remember,' Jessie Frazer put in.

'So we're not prison officers,' Frazer continued. 'We can't lock them up twenty-four hours a day. If a child is determined to run off, there's not a lot we can do to prevent it.'

The man had a good point, Jardine realised. He smiled apologetically. 'Yes, of course — I'm sorry,' he muttered. A sudden thought struck him. He turned to Jackie. 'Dunleath Woods,' he blurted out.

Jackie looked at him without understanding.

'That's where he'll be, I'd bet on it,' Jardine said, increasingly convinced that his guess had been right. 'He ran off there once before. It's where their father used to take them.'

'We'd better go and take a look,' Jackie suggested.

Brockwell smiled at them all patronisingly, as if he understood children far better than anyone and failed to understand the near-hysteria which seemed to be gripping everybody.

'They'll come home as soon as they're hungry,' he murmured. 'Children always do.'

Betty Duncan pushed a thick slice of cherry cake on to Nicola's plate. 'You haven't tried this yet,' she said, her tone faintly chiding.

Nicola shook her head, trying to push the plate away. 'I'm full up,' she complained.

Betty looked irritable. 'Nonsense, you've hardly eaten a thing. You can't be full up. Now eat up, the pair of you. I've made all this lovely food and you're not going to waste it.'

Simon looked at his sister's face and could see that she was on the point of crying. 'We're going to have to be going soon, anyway,' he said, trying to take the pressure of her.

Betty looked hurt, almost angry. 'You can't leave, not yet. Not until everything is eaten.'

Controlling her tears, Nicola tried to nibble at the piece of cherry cake. She was beginning to get a little frightened by the strange old woman.

Her fears were communicated to Simon. He racked his brains, trying to think of something which would take Betty's mind off her apparent obsession with food.

'Where's your husband?' he asked suddenly.

A faraway look stole over Betty's face. 'Oh, he left us a long, long time ago.'

'Why? Why did he leave?'

Betty looked at him in surprise. 'Why? Because he died, that's why.' She paused, reminiscing. 'He built this cottage out here in the woods so we could be away from the city. He didn't want other men to see me, you understand. I was very young, and very pretty then. Would you like to see me?'

Simon nodded, glad to have found something to distract her from Nicola and the unfinished food. Betty went to a drawer and rummaged about until she found an old framed photograph. She carried it across to Simon for his inspection.

The picture showed a young, very attractive Betty in her early twenties, standing beside a man who was many years older.

'He was a baker,' Betty went on. 'He taught me everything.' She broke off to sigh. 'He was a good man. He made an honest woman out of me.'

Simon felt the call of nature. 'Can I go to the toilet?' he asked politely.

Betty gestured up the stairs. 'It's up there, at the top of the stairs.' She walked over to Nicola, who was still struggling with the cherry cake, as Simon headed off to find the toilet.

'Your brother told me you like stories,' she said to the girl. 'What's your favourite?'

Nicola regarded her uncertainly, not sure if she was going to be bullied into eating again. 'Hansel and Gretel,' she said.

Betty's eyes gleamed. 'Well, next time you come, I'll bake a proper gingerbread house for you. Would you like that? It will have a real witch and a real Hansel and Gretel . . .'

She broke off suddenly as movement outside the window caught her eye. A large black dog was scratching and digging furiously in the ground beside the incinerator bin. Her face darkened. She raced for the back door, throwing it open and shouting at the dog.

'Get away, get away from there!' She stooped down and picked up a large stone, hurling it in the dog's direction. Tail between its legs, the dog jumped away from the incinerator and ran off into the woods. Betty continued to chase after it until she was completely satisfied that she had scared it off once and for all.

Upstairs, Simon was confronted with two doors. He tried the handle of the first, surprised to find that it was locked. It seemed odd, somehow, locking upstairs doors. As though there was some dark secret to hide. He tried the second door, relieved to find the toilet.

Afterwards he washed his hands in the small sink and dried them on a clean towel. He turned round, freezing as he saw what was hanging from a hook on the inside of the toilet door.

It was a blue rain cape with a hood.

Simon stared at it for several moments, his legs paralysed with shock and fear. Then the thought of his sister alone with Betty galvanised him into action again.

Simon dashed past the blue cape and ran down the stairs. Nicola sat alone at the table, Betty nowhere to be seen. Simon's eyes darted round the kitchen, noting the open back door. He pulled Nicola away from the table hurriedly.

'Come on, we have to go,' he hissed urgently.

The child did not protest as he hauled her towards the open door. Hand in hand, the two children ran across the back yard to where Simon had left his bike.

Simon had already perched Nicola on the crossbar and was preparing to pedal off as Betty re-emerged from the undergrowth. 'Sorry, we've got to go home now,' he called to her, as she stood looking disappointedly in their direction.

'But you will come back and see me again?' Betty pleaded with him.

'Of course.' Simon turned the wheel of the bike away from her, stepping on the pedal.

'You promise?' Betty called out anxiously, as the children began to head for the nearby lane.

They were just coming out on to the main road when Jardine and Jackie Reid intercepted them. Jardine stamped on the brakes and wound the car window down.

'Have you got any idea of the trouble you cause people?' he asked wearily as Simon stopped by the side of the car.

Chapter Fourteen

It was like the Spanish Inquisition, Simon thought. Confess your guilt so we can execute you, or we'll execute you for not confessing.

He sat in the Frazers' lounge, facing Jardine, Jackie Reid and Mr Frazer, in trouble with all of them. Jessie Frazer and Brockwell sat on the sidelines like a pair of impartial judges.

'I *did* see it,' Simon protested vociferously. 'It was a blue cape with a hood. It was hanging on the back of the bathroom door. It was the same cape, I'm sure of it.'

'You were just as sure that Mrs Frazer's brother was the killer,' Jardine pointed out.

Simon lowered his eyes. 'That was a mistake.'

'And the other time — when you thought you saw Mrs Duncan getting out of her car? I investigated that,' Jardine said. 'She has a *green* raincoat — she showed it to me.'

Simon refused to accept defeat. 'She could have two,' he suggested.

Jardine sighed. 'Simon, just tell me why you think an

elderly woman would want to kill your father.'

The boy was silent for a while. 'I don't know,' he admitted finally.

Frazer looked at him sympathetically. 'Simon, we know that you're upset and disturbed by what happened, and that's perfectly understandable. But you can't keep running off like this and coming back with wild stories. The next time you want to go and see this lady, just tell us first. That's all we ask.'

Simon looked pressurised and totally forlorn. Jardine felt a wave of sympathy for him. 'Remember what I told you about being a good detective, Simon? You need imagination, but not too much.'

Simon looked up at him with a plea for understanding in his eyes. 'I didn't imagine anything,' he said quietly. 'I know what I saw.'

'What you *thought* you saw,' Jardine corrected him gently. 'You've been through a terrible experience, Simon — an experience that should never happen to a boy your age. And, for the most part, you've coped with it incredibly well. But it's bound to have affected you, perhaps made you want to see things that just aren't there.' Jardine paused. 'What I'm trying to say, Simon, is that we all understand, really.'

Simon listened to Jardine carefully, with an expression of trust in his eyes. The haunted, pressurised look on his face gradually faded. Finally, he looked uncertain. 'Well, even if I did make a mistake, she's not just a harmless old woman,' he muttered. 'She's mad. She made us all this food and expected us to eat it.'

'Maybe she's just lonely,' Jackie Reid suggested.

'Or maybe she's a witch,' Simon retorted, only half-serious.

Brockwell broke his silence. 'There are no witches, Simon,' he said gently. 'There is magic, but no witches.'

Jardine rose to his feet. 'Look, we have to go, Simon. Are you all right now?'

The boy nodded. 'Do you really think I'm just seeing things?'

Jardine shrugged. 'I don't know, Simon. I just don't know,' he admitted truthfully.

Jackie Reid followed him to the door, saying nothing until they were back outside in the privacy of the car.

'A penny for them,' she murmured, seeing the perturbed look on Jardine's face.

Jardine sighed. 'It's just that however hard I am on him he still seems to look upon me as some sort of father figure,' he said.

'And how do you look on him?'

Jardine grinned ruefully. 'At the moment, as a perfect nuisance.'

Jackie started the car. 'I'd have thought you were feeling much more paternal lately,' she observed with a knowing smile.

Jardine let the crack pass without comment.

Taggart tapped lightly on the door of McVitie's office and opened the door without waiting for an invitation to enter. He was slightly surprised to find Gemma Normanton already ensconced in position, her skirt pulled up over her unmistakably attractive legs as she sat taking shorthand notes on a small steno pad.

McVitie waved a hand vaguely in the air, motioning Taggart to wait. Feeling a trifle awkward, Taggart hovered just inside the door while McVitie continued talking.

'Of course, what put us on the track of Bowman was his contact lens,' McVitie was saying. 'You may not know it, my dear, but an optician can look at a lens in much the same way that a dentist can look at a piece of bridge work and say, "That's my work". The professional touch, you see.'

'And who found the contact lens?' Gemma asked.

'One of his victims. She put it in her own eye, thinking it was one of hers that she'd dropped. But, of course, I realised the significance of it.'

McVitie broke off, looking over at Taggart. 'Yes, Jim? Anything important, or can it wait?'

The man could not have made it more obvious that he did

not want to be disturbed while had an attractive young woman to himself. Taggart shuffled a sheaf of papers in his hand awkwardly. 'It can wait, sir,' he muttered, backing out of the door again. Outside McVitie's office he stood still for a few seconds, fighting to control a sense of anger and outrage. He failed completely. A black look on his face, he stormed out into the main office just as Jardine and Jackie Reid were coming in.

Taggart in totally indignant mode was a phenomenon difficult to miss — or to ignore.

'Something wrong, sir?' Jardine enquired solicitously.

Taggart glowered at him. 'Aye, there's something wrong.' He jerked his thumb in the direction of McVitie's office. 'He's in there taking the credit for one of my cases. Putting himself at the centre of things.'

Jardine had to fight hard not to smile. Taggart's face was a study of righteous indignation and wounded pride. Instead, he forced an expression of concern on his face. 'That really takes the biscuit, sir, doesn't it?'

Seizing on the chance of a sympathetic ear, Taggart opened his mouth to go into details. 'But he's making out it was *his* case, and that *he* solved it.'

With a bit of quick thinking Jardine made a dive for his desk and picked up a small pile of papers. Returning to Jackie Reid he grabbed her by the arm and began to propel her towards the door.

'Anyway, can't stop,' he called over his shoulder to Taggart. 'We're due in Edinburgh to see the mother of another missing person.'

Taggart gaped after him, paranoid delusions of conspiracy forming in his mind. Finally, totally frustrated, he stormed into his office and slammed the door behind him.

Mrs Scott was somewhere in her early fifties, Jardine figured, as she opened the front door and regarded them both curiously.

'You'll be the two police people from Glasgow,' the woman said. 'I must admit I was rather surprised to receive your phone call after so long. Even more surprised to find that suddenly everybody is taking so much interest.'

'Everybody?' Jardine echoed blankly.

Mrs Scott stood back, motioning for them to enter. 'You'd better come in. Your colleague got here some time ago.'

Somewhat mystified, Jardine and Jackie followed her into the front room.

Bobby Gault rose from his armchair beside the fire as they walked into the room.

'This is Chief Inspector Gault of the Edinburgh police,' Mrs Scott said to Jardine.

'I know, we've met,' Jackie put in, concealing her surprise. She introduced Gault to Jardine, who shook the man's hand briefly. 'Sir.'

'Well, it's obvious that we're all here for the same reason,' Gault said briskly, taking charge. 'I have all the information we need, so I don't think we need upset Mrs Scott any further.'

'You're not upsetting me,' Mrs Scott said calmly. 'Just confusing me. So why this sudden show of concern? My son went missing nearly eighteen months ago and nobody seemed to want to do anything about it then. Now I have two police forces in my house, and I want to know why.'

Jardine cast an enquiring glance towards Gault, not sure of what to say, if anything at all. Gault shrugged faintly.

'Some recent developments have given us reason to open up some old missing person files,' Jardine said after a moment's thought. Diplomatically, he made no mention of murder. Mrs Scott obviously still thought of her son as absconded for reasons of his own. 'Other than that, there's really not much I can tell you.'

'And there might possibly be a connection between Edinburgh and Glasgow,' Gault put in. 'That's why we are working in conjunction with one another.'

Mrs Scott regarded them both intently for a while, finally

sighing. 'You're not going to tell me anything, are you?' she muttered in a slightly bitter tone. 'It's just like it was before. No one really wants to know.'

Jackie stepped forward to comfort the woman, offer her at least some hope. 'Please believe me, Mrs Scott — we're doing everything we can to find out what happened to your son. We just need to update our information, that's all.'

'For instance, this business about the telephone call,' Jardine said. 'Your son was nineteen years old. It seems odd that he should phone you up just to say he would be late home. Out of character for a teenager, somehow.'

Mrs Scott shook her head. 'Not at all. Ian was — is — a very responsible boy. He knew we worried about him.'

'And the reason for the call. Ian said he was going for a drink with friends. Did he say which friends? Our initial investigations failed to turn up anyone Ian knew in Glasgow.'

Mrs Scott shrugged. 'We didn't know all his friends. Ian is a popular boy. It could have been someone from here, someone he met in the theatre during the interval.'

'Was it something he did regularly — phone you to say what he was doing?' Jardine asked.

Mrs Scott thought for a while. 'No, now you come to mention it,' she admitted finally. 'It wasn't something he'd ever done before.'

Gault couldn't see the point of Jardine's questions. 'Look, I really think we have all the information we need for the moment,' he interrupted, sounding slightly irritable. 'I think it's best if we leave Mrs Scott alone now.'

It was a thinly veiled order. Another police force or not, Gault was their superior. Jardine had no choice but to obey. He thanked Mrs Scott for her time and reluctantly followed Gault to the front door.

They were hardly over the threshold before the reason for Gault's urgent need to get out of the house became clear. Jardine smiled thinly as the man dipped into his pocket, took a blue cigarette out of his case and lit it, sucking in the smoke with the slavish devotion of a true addict.

'What was all that business about the telephone call?' Gault wanted to know as they walked down the drive.

'Mike has a theory,' Jackie put in brightly.

Jardine shook his head slowly. 'It's not really a theory. Just an observation, really. Archie Ross phoned home about a birthday present for his son. Ian Scott called his mother to say he would be going for a late drink. Frank Innes rang to tell his wife he loved her.'

Gault rubbed at his chin reflectively. 'And Phillip Chalmers phoned Elsa with a similar message,' he mused thoughtfully. 'I agree, there does seem to be some sort of pattern. What do you make of it?'

Jardine shrugged. 'Nothing, at the moment,' he admitted. 'As I said, it's only an observation.'

Gault thought for a few more seconds, unable to come up with any suggestions himself. 'Look, tell your boss I'll contact him in the morning,' he said finally. Puffing away at his cigarette he strode off towards his car.

Jardine glanced sideways at Jackie. 'What's he doing on this case if he's so personally involved?' he wanted to know.

She raised one eyebrow querulously. 'I don't know — but it *is* his patch.'

Jardine was unconvinced. 'Even so, there's something about that man I don't quite trust,' he observed.

Jackie grinned. 'Who could possibly trust a man who smokes blue cigarettes?'

Jardine smiled back at her. 'Perhaps it adds colour to his love life.'

Laughing, they returned to their car.

Taggart sat in his office with the door open, his eyes fixed on McVitie's private sanctum. He was calmer now, after a full afternoon and evening of routine work to occupy his mind, but he still wanted to talk to him, perhaps find some discreet way of expressing his chagrin.

McVitie's door opened eventually. The man came out in

the process of putting on his coat. Taggart moved quickly to intercept him.

'Going over the road for a drink, sir?' he asked innocently.

McvVitie shook his head. 'Not tonight, Jim. Promised I'd get home early to play a rubber of bridge with Marjory and some of her bowling friends.'

Taggart hid his disappointment under a thin smile. 'Have a nice evening.' He fell into step with his superior as he walked out of the office. 'Did you have a good meeting with Miss Normanton?" he asked casually.

McVitie's eyes twinkled. 'What a charming young woman,' he observed. 'You should talk to her, Jim. She's like a breath of fresh air.'

They reached the exit. McVitie paused briefly, glancing at Taggart.

'Anything on Gingerbread Men?'

Taggart shook his head. 'Nothing yet.' He thought aloud for a moment. 'Perhaps it's two separate words, not connected. Gingerbread. And men.'

McVitie looked dubious. 'Or just the ramblings of a dying man,' he muttered. 'Are you totally convinced we're on the right track with these other missing person cases?'

'It's all we have to go on at the moment, sir,' Taggart said bluntly.

McVitie buttoned his coat. 'Just remember that the murdered man was a private detective. There could be dozens of people with a grievance. We don't want to shunt ourselves into a siding.'

He stepped out into the street and began to walk away.

'Good night, sir,' Taggart muttered, turning in the opposite direction. Alone, he headed across the road towards the pub.

The pub was virtually empty. It appeared to be one of those nights when everyone had something better to do, Taggart thought moodily. And just when he needed some male company, someone to talk to. So it was with a sense of relief that he recognised the familiar figure of Dr Andrews standing at the bar. Taggart approached him thankfully.

'Hello, Stephen. What can I get you?' he asked.

Andrews glanced sideways at him, a look of regret on his face. It wasn't every day that Taggart offered to buy the drinks. 'Sorry, Jim, but we're just about to leave.'

At that moment Gemma Normanton came out of the ladies' room and walked across to join them.

'I'm taking Gemma out for a meal and to talk about the Samson case,' Andrews explained.

Taggart digested this information stoically. 'The Samson case, eh?'

'I was just telling Gemma that, forensically, it was one of the most fascinating cases I ever worked on.,' Andrews went on. 'That page-three girl in the burnt-out boat, the shotgun killing of John Samson and the near cremation of the father with that drug succinylchloride inside him.'

Gemma smiled up at Taggart sweetly. 'Mike told me that you were in charge of that case.'

Taggart nodded. 'I was,' he said, with an extra bit of emphasis for Andrews' benefit. He might have said more but Andrews pre-empted him.

'Well, come along young lady. That restaurant table was booked for ten minutes ago.'

Gemma smiled apologetically at Taggart. 'Well, perhaps we can talk some other time,' she suggested. 'Good night.'

'Good night.' Taggart turned away, facing over the bar to order a double whisky and hide the gloomy expression on his face.

Deprived of colleagues or male friends, there was only Jean, and even she didn't seem too interested in his troubles. Taggart lay in bed, sulking, as his wife sat up reading a book.

'They were *my* cases,' he complained bitterly. 'Cases that *I* solved. Now it seems that everybody else is jumping in to claim the credit for them.'

Jean laid her book down with a faint sigh. It was obvious that he wasn't going to leave her in peace until she had offered him some show of support.

'Well, you refused to speak to her, so what did you expect?' she pointed out to him.

'A bit of credit where credit's due.'

'Well, there's a very simple answer.' Jean didn't bother to spell it out for him.

Taggart shook his head miserably. 'I've already nailed my colours to the mast.'

'Then un-nail them,' Jean said simply.

It wasn't really the answer Taggart wanted to hear. He turned to her. 'Jean, I've seen these kind of books. They're unhealthy. People read them for a sordid thrill, not because they're really interested in detective work. Besides, I haven't got the time to talk to her.'

His wife shot that argument down at once. 'Nonsense. You've plenty of time.'

'In the middle of a case?' Taggart demanded.

Jean shrugged. 'Well, everyone else seems to find some time. Jack McVitie, Dr Andrews, Michael. Especially Michael, it seems.'

Taggart changed the subject abruptly, realising he was fighting a losing battle. 'All I want is a break. The meaning of Gingerbread Men.'

Jean reached up to switch off her overhead reading light. 'You'll get it,' she said confidently. 'You always do.'

Taggart looked across at her, the faintest trace of a smile crossing his face for the first time that evening. 'Such confidence.'

'No, a bit of credit,' his wife murmured. 'A bit of credit for you to go to *sleep* with.'

She turned over and buried her face in the pillow.

Chapter Fifteen

The black dog scrabbled furiously at its favourite burial patch at the bottom of the garden, eager to retrieve one of its treasures. A couple of old and dry lamb bones were unearthed, sniffed at and finally rejected before the dog found something far more interesting. Its tail wagging happily, it grasped the object firmly between its teeth and trotted up the garden towards the house to show off its find to its loving master.

Dave Jobson paid the dog no attention as it trotted into the living-room. His eyes were firmly glued to the television set. Can of beer in one hand, and cigarette in the other, he concentrated on the ongoing snooker match, willing Steve Davis to miss the shot he was currently lining up on the blue ball.

Mind over matter lost out completely as Davis potted the blue and brought the cue ball spinning back for a perfect shot on one of the last loose reds. Jobson muttered a curse, knowing that the frame was now more or less sewn up, and that his five pound bet on Jimmy White was now a lost cause.

Mistaking the sound of its beloved master's voice for an expression of endearment, the dog trotted over and nudged his leg, seeking his attention. Proudly it dropped the object between its jaws by his feet and looked up at him, its eyes gleaming.

Jobson stubbed out the last half inch of his cigarette into the ashtray and reached down absently to stroke the dog's black head. The animal whined gently, demanding more direct attention. Finally, with a faintly indulgent smile, Jobson tore his attention away from the TV screen and glanced down at his pet.

His eyes fell upon the object nestling by his feet. Jobson's initial shock and revulsion were quickly followed by a cold shudder of horror as he recognised the revolting piece of rotting flesh for what it was.

Badly burned, chewed up and in an advanced state of decomposition, the thing was still clearly identifiable as a severed human hand.

Dr Andrews poked at the dismembered object now gracing McVitie's desk with a pair of surgical forceps and a spatula.

'It's in an advanced state of decomposition,' he announced, rather superfluously. Both McVitie and Taggart had noses which had long since made this fact quite apparent. 'Most of the flesh is gone, and there's evidence of post-mortem burning and burial.'

'Could you still get prints off it?' Taggart asked hopefully.

'The Moving Finger Writes, Jim,' Andrews murmured, for no apparent reason.

Andrews lifted the hand up with the forceps and studied what was left of the fingers through a magnifying glass. He glanced up at Taggart, nodding faintly. 'I'd say it was quite possible. They managed to get identifiable prints from John Dillinger even after he'd attempted to burn them off with sulphuric acid.'

'Dillinger?' McVitie queried.

'American gangster, sir,' Taggart informed him.

'Ah.' McVitie lapsed into silence.

'Anyway, the point I was trying to make was that finger-prints are quite difficult things to destroy,' Andrews went on. 'Even under rotting flesh.'

Taggart looked pleased. He had not really expected a positive answer to his question. 'Well, can you get it down to the lab and make a start?' he wanted to know. 'I'm going to talk to the man who brought it in — wrapped up in his handkerchief, would you believe?'

Andrews nodded. 'Right away, Jim.' He picked up the hand gently with the forceps and dropped it into the clear plastic bag.

McVitie looked greatly relieved to have it off his desk. He glanced up at Taggart. 'You'll keep me informed?'

'Of course, sir.' Taggart followed Andrews out of McVitie's office and headed for his own, where Jardine and Jackie Reid had just finished taking Dave Jobson's statement.

Jobson looked up expectantly as Taggart walked in. 'Have you found out who it belongs to?' he wanted to know.

Taggart shot him a withering look. 'Well, no one's turned up to claim it yet,' he muttered sarcastically.

'Mr Jobson was just telling us that his dog is in the habit of wandering off for days at a time and bringing things back to bury in the garden,' Jackie informed him.

'How far does he go?' Taggart asked.

Jobson shrugged. 'He's never told me,' he said, paying Taggart back.

Taggart let it go. 'What sort of a dog is it?'

'He's only a collie cross,' Jobson said defensively. 'I mean, he's not a dangerous dog or anything like that. He wouldn't have bitten it off anybody.'

'That's reassuring to know,' Taggart muttered, glaring at the man and wondering whether he was trying to take the mickey or merely a bit thick.

Jardine jumped in to bring the conversation back to a

more constructive level. 'Our neighbour's dog used to wander off for fifteen, even twenty miles or so.'

Taggart looked glum. 'Great,' he muttered. 'So we only have the whole of Glasgow to search.'

'I suppose we'd better start with Mr Jobson's back garden,' Jackie suggested helpfully. 'See if there is any other buried treasure.'

It was the logical starting point — and one that Taggart himself would have suggested if he hadn't got into verbal fencing with Jobson. He nodded briefly at Jackie. 'Organise a digging team and meet me there in half an hour,' he snapped. He turned his attention to Jardine. 'We could be in luck. Dr Andrews seems to think he might still get prints off that thing.'

Jardine nodded thoughtfully. 'They're very hard things to destroy,' he started to say. 'Did you know the American police even managed to take Dillinger's prints even after —'

'He'd burned them off with acid,' Taggart finished for him. 'Yes, I know.' He took a slight satisfaction from the deflated expression on his young colleague's face.

Two hours of intensive excavation work had reduced Jobson's back garden to a wasteland of freshly turned earth and uprooted shrubs. Jobson, and his dog, regarded the mess moodily.

'He just goes off when the mood takes him,' Jobson was saying. 'I mean, it's not a regular thing. Sometimes he won't wander off for weeks, then you'll turn your back for a minute and he's gone — sometimes for two or three days.'

Taggart digested this information thoughtfully. 'So we have to wait around indefinitely before we can follow him?'

'I've a much better idea, sir,' Jackie put in brightly. 'Couldn't we get the surveillance unit to fit him with a homing device on his collar, or something like that?'

It was a brilliant idea, Taggart had to concede. 'Then *you* could wait around to follow him. You're right — that is a good idea.'

Jackie wished she had kept her mouth shut. That wasn't quite what she'd had in mind.

Jardine called over to them from where he had been supervising the digging team. 'Well, this seems about the lot, sir.'

Taggart and Jackie strolled over to where a number of buried objects had been unearthed and sorted into separate groups. One pile contained various animal bones and assorted objects. The second group was a grisly collection of clearly human remains.

'One human right foot, part of another hand with two fingers — and something unidentifiable,' Jardine said, indicating each object in turn.

Jackie Reid looked at the piece of rotting flesh Jardine had called 'unidentifiable' and managed a grim smile. 'You don't have to resort to euphemisms for my benefit, you know. I'm a big girl now.'

Jobson's dog sniffed anxiously at the various body parts, worrying them with one of its paws.

Taggart called over the Dave Jobson. 'Could you get over here and get this dog of yours under control?'

Jobson strolled over, looked at the assorted body pieces and smiled down at his dog. 'You've been a busy boy, haven't you, Rusty?' he said with more than a trace of pride in his voice.

Taggart glowered at him as he hooked his fingers under the dog's collar and dragged it away towards the house.

'We don't know for sure if it's Phillip Chalmers,' Jardine observed. 'Or any of our other missing persons for that matter.'

'Hopefully we'll know soon enough,' Taggart said. 'There must still be prints left in his house, even after two months.'

Jackie Reid pointed down at the foot. 'That foot looks too fresh to have been buried for two months, sir,' she pointed out.

GINGERBREAD

Taggart looked at it more carefully. She was right, he had to admit. He was about to say something when Jobson called from the house.

'Mr Taggart — there's a telephone call for you.'

Taggart headed for the house at a loping run. Jobson handed him the phone. It was McVitie.

'I wouldn't bother you on the job ordinarily, Jim,' McVitie said. 'But it looks as though we might have another missing person who fits the pattern. A James Buchanan, travelling salesman from Newcastle. Phoned his wife two days ago to say he'd be home in the morning and never showed up. Our records show his car was found abandoned and clamped near Central Station yesterday morning.'

'I'll get on to it, sir,' Taggart said and hung up the phone. He crossed to the window, opened it and called out to Jardine and Jackie. 'Get in here, the pair of you. I've got a job for you.'

Buchanan's car opened easily after only three attempts with a small bunch of skeleton keys.

Jackie Reid shook her head ruefully. 'No wonder there are so many car thefts,' she observed. She pulled the driver's door fully open and reached over to the other side to unlock the passenger door for Jardine. They peered inside the car, noting the pile of samples and presentation packs on the rear seat.

'Doesn't look as though much has been taken,' Jardine said. 'So theft obviously wasn't the motive.'

'And the car looks totally undamaged, which would be unusual if it were joyriders,' Jackie observed.

Jardine picked up a card from the dashboard. 'It looks like he played bingo.' He noted that the numbers were all crossed off. 'And got a full house from the look of it.'

Jackie had made her own discovery. Looking down at the driver's seat, she noticed a small pile of brownish crumbs. Moistening the tip of one finger with her tongue, she dabbed at one of the larger crumbs, picking it up and holding it to her nose, sniffing. She looked at Jardine, a surprised look on her face. 'Gingerbread?'

Jardine leaned over to examine the seat more carefully.

'Why don't you taste one to make sure?' Jackie suggested.

'Don't need to,' Jardine said suddenly. He reached down by the side of the driver's seat where something had dropped down between the seat frame and the handbrake. He picked it up carefully, holding it up for her inspection.

It was the broken-off head of a gingerbread man, with currants for its eyes.

Chapter Sixteen

Gavin, the bingo hall drag queen, was putting the finishing touches to his make-up in preparation for the first house of the evening. One of the ticker-sellers poked her blonde head around the door.

'Visitors for you.' She showed Taggart, Jardine and Jackie Reid into the tiny dressing-room.

Gavin eyed Jardine appreciatively, his false eyelashes fluttering. 'Well, it's lovely to see you, dear, but I have a show in five minutes.'

Taggart regarded the camp little man with an expression of vague disapproval. 'We're not your fan club,' he snapped, pulling out his ID card and introducing himself. He thrust a photograph of Jimmy Buchanan under Gavin's nose. 'This man — was he in here a couple of nights ago?'

Gavin gave the photo a cursory glance, recognising Buchanan at once. 'I can't be expected to remember everyone who comes in here,' he muttered evasively.

Taggart's face hardened. 'Now, look — you have two

121

TAGGART

choices here. Either you tell us now or we can put you in a holding cell until you *do* remember. Apart from missing your grand performance, some of the drunks and roughnecks we pull in tonight might have some very interesting reactions to someone like you.'

Gavin could not fail to understand the implications. He looked at the photograph again, nodding. 'He was in here on Tuesday night. Won a hundred and fifty quid.'

'And where did he go afterwards? Do you know?'

Gavin nodded again. 'I saw him later in the pub up the road. The Stirling Castle.'

'Was he alone?' Jardine asked.

Gavin flashed him a knowing smile. 'You're only alone in that place if you want to be. He was with two women.'

'Can you describe them?'

Gavin shrugged his shoulders in an expansive gesture. 'What's to describe? Working girls. One blonde, one black haired. Jenny and Ann, they're called.'

Jackie Reid had been eyeing up the selection of wigs and frocks lying around the dressing-room. 'Mind if I pass on a little feminine tip?' she said sweetly.

Gavin preened, looking at her. 'What's that?'

'Your eyeliner's smudged.' Grinning wickedly she turned to join Taggart and Jardine as they headed for the door.

The tall, elegant figure of Bobby Gault greeted them as they walked out into the street. He pushed himself away from the wall where he had been leaning, brushing the shoulder of his jacket with an exaggerated gesture. He gave Taggart one of his slightly superior smiles.

Taggart was less than pleased to see him. 'What are you doing here?' he demanded brusquely.

Gault paused to light a red cigarette. 'I got here as soon as I heard.'

'Heard what?' Taggart demanded.

'Our sweet-toothed driver strikes again,' Gault murmured.

Taggart scowled at him. 'We don't know there's a connection yet. Just don't get under my feet.' He strode up the street towards the Stirling Castle pub, making it perfectly clear that this was *his* patch, and he was in charge.

He stopped outside the pub entrance, regarding Gault's cigarette with a slightly mocking look. 'I wouldn't smoke a red cigarette in here if I were you. You're likely to get lynched.'

Gault peered inside the pub, noted the rough and ready clientele and got the message. Reluctantly he dropped the cigarette to the pavement and stubbed it out with the heel of his shoe.

Taggart led the way in. He pushed through the crowd of drinkers clustered around the bar.

'Two regular girls — Jenny and Ann. Are they in tonight?' he demanded of the barman.

The man nodded over to where the two women sat at a table.

Ann Kirk saw the little group heading towards the table and nudged Jenny warningly. 'Law,' she muttered, her instincts honed by years of experience. 'Just keep your mouth shut and let me do the talking.'

She looked up at Taggart as he approached, a hard, defiant look on her face.

'Are you Jenny and Ann?' Taggart asked.

Ann jerked her thumb sideways. 'She's Jenny.'

'We're from Maryhill Police Station,' Jackie Reid told her.

Ann's eyes were cold, motionless. 'I thought you might be from somewhere.'

Taggart laid the photograph of Buchanan down on the table. 'Were you in the company of this man on Tuesday night?'

Ann glanced down at the picture, poker-faced. With practised disinterest she looked up at Taggart coolly, knowing the form. Too late, she remembered Jenny and kicked her ankle under the table, but the young girl had already recognised Buchanan and given the game away with a gasp of surprise.

The inexperienced girl's reaction had been enough for Taggart.

'We'd like you to accompany us down to the station.' It was an order, not a request.

Ann became more openly aggressive. 'Why?' she demanded.

'Because he's gone missing,' Taggart said simply.

Ann glared at him. 'Bloody coppers,' she spat out. She picked her handbag up from the table and vented her anger on Jenny. 'Thanks. That's another night's business ruined.'

The girl looked as though she was about to cry. Ann's face softened, feeling sorry for her. She looked at Taggart again, her defiant attitude tempered with almost matronly concern. 'Look, she's just a kid. She's all right. Give her a break, eh?'

Taggart reached down to help Jenny to her feet. 'How old are you, Jenny?' he asked in a not unkindly tone.

The girl spoke for the first time. 'Eighteen.'

Taggart glared wordlessly at Ann Kirk, but his expression was accusatory, speaking volumes.

The woman bristled defensively. 'Look, I'm not pimping for her, or anything like that. I look out for her. Some of the punters like the schoolgirl look, you know?'

Taggart was unconvinced. 'Quite the little mother hen, aren't we? You think kids this age should be out on the streets?'

Ann Kirk flashed him an almost pitying look. 'You don't know anything, do you?' she asked. 'You've got no bloody idea, you coppers.' She looked scathingly at Gault, who was hovering on the sidelines. 'Look at fancypants there. I bet he's still looking for Raffles, the gentleman thief.'

Gault looked vaguely embarrassed, out of his depth. The seamy side of Glasgow's night life was a far cry from bone china crockery and Earl Grey tea.

Jackie Reid had taken charge of Jenny McClusky, escorting her away from the table with an arm around the young girl's shoulders. Taggart smiled inwardly at Ann Kirk's observation. The woman was hard as nails, but she had a point.

'You say you look out for Jenny,' Taggart said to her. 'Why?'

The woman faced him squarely, a grim smile on her face. 'Because I know what can happen out there, that's why.' She pulled her black hair away from the side of her face, displaying her cheek. A livid white scar ran from just under her left eye all the way to her chin. 'See that? A pimp gave me that years ago. Business hasn't been quite the same since, you might say.'

Taggart looked away. It wasn't a pretty sight.

'Anyway, that's why I took the number of the car Jenny and that guy went off in,' Ann finished.

'Have you still got it?' Jardine asked.

By way of answer, the woman fished in her handbag and pulled out a small notebook. She flipped it to the last page, tore the sheet out and handed it to him. 'They didn't do anything, anyway,' she muttered.

'How do you know that?' Taggart wanted to know.

Ann gave him another withering look. 'Because she told me. This one was a gentleman.'

Jenny was nervous and tearful. It was probably the first time she had been picked up by the police, Taggart figured. For much the same reason his instincts told him that she was probably telling the truth.

He and Gault took it easy on the girl, putting their questions simply and gently to her.

'So — after Buchanan drove off with you, what happened?' Taggart asked.

'We went up near the new link road and parked,' the girl answered. 'Then we just sat in the car and talked.'

'And what else, Jenny?' Taggart prompted.

For a prostitute the girl seemed remarkably naïve. 'What else?'

'What did you do?' Gault put in.

Jenny looked at them both, her eyes wide with innocence. 'Nothing else. We ate some chocolate, that's all.'

Taggart wondered briefly whether 'eating chocolate' was some new form of sexual deviation and decided that it wasn't. 'Chocolate, Jenny?' he queried.

The girl nodded. 'He was a rep for a confectionery firm. He had boxes of it on the back seat.'

'How about gingerbread?' Gault asked. 'Did either of you eat a gingerbread man?'

Jenny looked puzzled. 'A gingerbread man? No, there was nothing like that.'

'How about the words "gingerbread man". Or just "gingerbread"? Do they mean anything to you at all?' Taggart wanted to know.

The girl continued to look baffled. 'No.'

Taggart sighed. 'So, basically, Buchanan picked you up in a pub, knowing you were on the game, drove you to a lonely spot and then paid you just to sit with him and eat chocolate? Is that what you're telling us?'

The girls eyes blazed indignantly. 'He didn't pay me. I told you, we didn't do anything.'

Taggart was getting a little frustrated, but he held his patience. 'That doesn't make any sense, Jenny,' he pointed out. 'I think you're hiding something. What is it?'

Jenny's eyes flickered with guilt and embarrassment. She stared down at the floor as though ashamed to face Taggart directly. 'All right — he *did* ask me to do something,' she went on in a low, uncertain voice. 'But I told him I didn't like doing that sort of thing and he said it was all right, he understood. He said he had a young daughter himself, and he wouldn't like anyone trying to force her to do anything against her will. I told you, he was a nice man. A kind man.'

Taggart smiled ruefully to himself, seeing the young girl's obvious innocence. He wondered, sadly, how long it would be before she had it knocked out of her by the harsh realities of the sordid profession she had taken up.

'How long have been doing this, Jenny?' he asked gently.

'Two weeks,' the girl answered, and Taggart believed her.

'So what happened after you'd eaten chocolate?' he asked, getting back to the facts.

'We talked a bit more — then he drove me back to the pub and gave me five pounds for a couple of drinks.'

'And you didn't see him again?' Gault asked.

Jenny shook her head. 'Not until you showed me his picture tonight.'

Gault and Taggart exchanged a glance. As if by mutual consent they seemed to agree that there wasn't much point in continuing the interrogation.

Taggart stood up. 'All right, Jenny — you can go now, but we might need to talk to you again,' he said quietly.

He let Gault escort her to the door. As an afterthought Taggart called out to her as she walked away. 'Oh, Jenny — I think you picked the wrong job,' he told her. He felt better for saying it, even though he knew it probably wouldn't make a scrap of difference.

Chapter Seventeen

Simon cycled down the lane towards the cottage, a worried, slightly guilty look on his face. What he was doing was wrong, he knew — but there were questions which desperately needed answers and, apparently, no one able, or willing, to get them.

Within sight of the cottage, Simon dismounted, propping his bike against a tree. He stood looking at the cottage for some time, summoning his courage. Finally, taking a deep breath, he strode purposefully up to the front door and rapped with the knocker.

There was no answer for a long time. Simon waited on the front step, trembling slightly with fear and expectancy. Somewhere behind him, deep in the woods, he heard the grating buzz of a chainsaw starting up, which distracted his attention for a moment.

The door opened suddenly, making him jump. He took a step back as Betty Duncan stared out at him, at first in surprise and then in anger. Her hair was loose and lank, dropping wispily over her wrinkled features. Beneath the angry mask of her face her eyes registered something else, difficult to define. It could have been hate, Simon thought — or it could even have been fear. Whatever, the total effect was to make Betty seem even more evil and witch-like than normal. Simon's mouth dropped open slackly, but no words came out.

'Go away,' Betty hissed at him. 'I told you never, never to come here without phoning first. Now go — go away!'

The door slammed shut. Simon had already taken several more steps backwards, stunned by the intensity and fury of the old woman's outburst. Now he stood rooted with shock, unable to move. It was several seconds before he was able to turn from the door and stumble away into the woods.

Simon skirted through the trees and undergrowth, seeking a roundabout route back to where he had left his bike. Retrieving it, his legs still felt a little shaky, so he wheeled it off the cottage path through the woods towards the lane.

The buzz of the chainsaw became louder. Stepping into a small clearing, Simon saw Joe Soutar, the forestry worker, attacking the thick trunk of a felled tree. Catching sight of him, the man looked up from his work, switched off the saw and stared at Simon curiously.

In the abrupt silence, Simon heard the sound of an old and badly tuned car engine heading in his direction. He glanced aside to see Brockwell's old van bumping along the lane towards him. The van stopped and Brockwell climbed out.

'Jessie asked me to come and collect you,' Brockwell announced cheerily.

Simon glared at him resentfully. 'I don't need collecting.'

'And I thought it might be a good chance for me to meet your friend in the cottage,' Brockwell added.

Simon's frustration exploded in an angry outburst. 'She won't meet you. She won't meet anybody today. She's mad.'

'But I thought she liked to see you,' Brockwell said.

'She's quite mad,' Simon repeated. 'She said never to come without ringing — so I wanted to find out what she would do if I did. She was crazy. I thought she was going to attack me.'

Brockwell let the boy rant on for a while. 'Look, she's an old widow, living out here in the woods all alone,' he said finally. 'People can get a bit strange sometimes — a little eccentric.' He moved to open the rear doors of the van. 'Come on, Simon — let's put your bike in the back of the van and we'll go home.'

Simon let Brockwell pick up the bike and load it into the van. 'Why does no one believe me?' he asked plaintively.

Brockwell smiled faintly. 'What, about her being a witch?'

Simon shook his head. 'About her having something to do with my dad's murder,' he said with grim determination. He looked sideways as he spoke, suddenly aware that Soutar was still watching him and could probably overhear every word. An earlier fear, that Soutar was somehow in league with the old woman, resurfaced. Simon climbed into the van hastily as Brockwell locked up the rear doors.

'Just remember what Sergeant Jardine told you about too much imagination,' Brockwell muttered, climbing in beside him. 'And as for witches — well, maybe there are one or two. I suppose it wouldn't do to stop believing in such things altogether, would it?'

He started up the van and set it into motion with a crash of gears. As the vehicle moved off, Joe Soutar watched after it with a thoughtful expression on his face. Turning, he stared towards the cottage, just able to pick out Betty Duncan's face peering out through the window from behind the curtain.

Jackie Reid sat in Dave Jobson's front room, idly flipping through a book with a bored expression on her face. Jobson, as ever, sat in front of the television set, his eyes rivetted to the screen. The dog lay sprawled out on a mat in front of the fire, the homing device attached to its collar emitting a faint, pulsing red flash. The animal had remained in this position for the best part of three hours now, showing absolutely no inclination to wander anywhere.

Jackie peered over the top of her book, regarding the recumbent animal morosely. 'You don't think the flashing red light on that thing is putting him off, do you?' she asked.

Nigel Wynn-Davies, the young DC from the surveillance unit, shook his head. 'The LED is on the back — he's not aware of it,' he explained. 'And there's no sound, so it shouldn't affect the animal in any way.' He fell silent again, regarding the dog hopefully and nursing the electronic box of tricks in his lap.

The doorbell rang. Jackie sprang to her feet, glad of anything to relieve the monotony. 'I'll get it.'

She walked out, returning a few seconds later with Jardine.

'Well, how's Operation Walkies going?' he enquired brightly.

Jackie flashed him a pained expression, nodding at the dog. 'Does that answer your question?'

Jardine shivered suddenly. 'Hell of a draught in here,' he observed. 'Have you got a door open or something?'

'The back door,' Jackie said peevishly. 'We keep throwing him out into the back garden but he keeps trotting straight back in here.' She broke off, drawing Jardine's attention to Wynn-Davies. 'Oh, by the way — this is Nigel Wynn-Davies, from the surveillance unit.'

Jardine shook the young man's hand. 'So nothing happening yet?'

'Well, the homing device is in place and it's working perfectly. So, basically, all we can do is wait,' came the answer.

'And wait . . . and wait,' Jackie added with heavy emphasis.

'I was just saying to your colleague how advanced our techniques have become,' Wynn-Davies said to Jardine. 'We can keep the tracking line so precise now that the bug can be followed to within a few feet even from a distance of fifty miles.'

Jackie tried to bury herself in her book again, having heard the spiel at least a couple of times already. Wynn-Davies was a young man of singular devotion to the job. Other than that, he had absolutely no source of conversation.

'Usually it's vehicles with large sums of money on board or high-risk prisoners we have to monitor — so this job comes as quite a challenge,' Wynn-Davies went on. 'I'm finding it quite fascinating.'

'I'm bloody glad somebody is,' Jackie muttered in the background. She looked over at Jardine, an appeal in her eyes. 'I suppose you don't fancy giving me a couple of hours' break?'

Jardine smiled apologetically. 'Sorry, but I've got to get home. Gemma's waiting for me. I promised to take her to the Riverside Club.'

There was a momentary sign of life from the couch potato in front of the TV set. Jobson actually moved, thumping his fist against the arm of the chair. 'Bloody hell — Hendry's missed the pink!' he exclaimed, then fell silent again.

Jackie looked as though she were about to scream. She jumped to her feet, crossed to the snoozing dog and prodded it into life with the point of her show. 'Come on, you useless mutt. Get out there and give us all an exciting evening.'

The dog trotted round the room in a small circle, then returned to the mat in front of the fire, lying down with its head across its paws.

Jardine decided it was time for a tactical retreat. Aware of Jackie's eyes glaring at him, he made a discreet exit.

The flat was empty. There was no Gemma, no ready prepared drink after a day's work and no welcoming kiss. Just a note, stuck on the side of Gemma's word processor.

Jardine pulled it off and read the short message. His face creased into a frown. Screwing the note into a tight little ball, he tossed it into the waste-paper basket. He sank down into the nearest armchair, feeling frustrated and more than a little guilty about Jackie.

It was going to be a long and lonely evening for everybody.

Chapter Eighteen

Gemma Normanton raised her wine-glass in a toast. 'Cheers. It was very good of you to invite me to dinner like this.'

Taggart smiled at her over the top of the flickering table candles, sipping from his own glass. 'I thought it wasn't fair for you to write your book and then find you had some of your facts wrong.'

'The fact is, Jim has headed every major murder inquiry in Glasgow over the past eight years,' Jean Taggart put in. The dinner-party had been her idea, and she intended to see that it served its purpose well.

Taggart shrugged modestly. 'Och, I wouldn't say *every* one, Jean.'

His wife smiled somewhat wistfully. 'Well, maybe it just seems like that sometimes.'

Gemma picked at her food delicately. 'I have a lot of questions to ask you. So I really am grateful for this opportunity.'

Taggart regarded her steadily over the table. 'First of all, though, I'd like to put you right about two key facts. Firstly, in the Samson case, I suggested to Dr Andrews that John Samson's death was murder. The victim had been killed or stunned with a blow to the head, then the shotgun fired through the mouth, effectively obliterating any other sign of injury. It was meant to look like a suicide, you see. It was nearly the perfect murder.'

Gemma digested this piece of information along with her boeuf bourguignon. 'And the second?'

'Who have you been told discovered the contact lens clue in the Bowman case?'

Gemma smiled knowingly. 'Ah, well. I know that Superintendent McVitie tried to take the credit for it, but it was really Mike, of course.'

Taggart nearly choked on a forkful of meat. 'Mike! Whatever gave you that idea?'

Gemma looked uncertain. 'Wasn't it?'

'Mike Jardine had only just joined us at the time of the Bowman case,' Taggart hastened to point out. 'He was only a DC then.'

'Jim was the first person to realise the significance of that contact lens,' Jean said, putting the record straight. 'Bowman lost it in one of his victim's houses and she put it into her own eye, thinking it was one of hers. But, of course, she couldn't see clearly — a fact which Jim picked up on right away.'

'In fact, Mike was only a very small cog in that particular investigation,' Taggart added, stressing the point.

Gemma grinned over at him. 'You know, I think this evening is going to be very informative,' she mused.

'You'll have to tell Gemma about the dismembered drug dealer case as well,' Jean Taggart suggested. 'How you had all those body parts but couldn't find the head.'

Taggart paused in his eating, staring thoughtfully at the large chunk of meat on the end of his fork. 'Actually, I thought we might leave that one until after dinner,' he muttered.

Jenny McClusky looked moodily around the scruffy little flat she shared with Ann Kirk. It was cheap, shoddy and slovenly, she thought — a long way away from the luxurious and fancy boudoirs of the high-priced call-girls and great courtesans she had once dreamed of emulating. Perhaps Taggart had been right, she pondered. Perhaps she had picked the wrong job.

He had seemed a decent man. Brusque, perhaps, but essentially kind-hearted. Strangely, Taggart reminded her of her father in some ways. She found it hard to share Ann's totally cynical view that because he was a copper he had to be some sort of a bastard. In fact, there was a lot about the older woman's viewpoint on life that Jenny found hard to accept. But she had come to a strange, lonely city needing someone, and Ann Kirk had been available.

The telephone rang. Ann pushed herself to her feet, a faint look of hope on her normally sullen face. 'I'll get it,' she announced. 'With a bit of luck it'll be a customer.'

She walked to the phone and answered it, the optimism fading from her face quickly. She held the phone out at arm's length, calling to the younger girl. 'It's for you. Some bloke calling himself Ginger.'

Jenny rose to her feet without much enthusiasm. She thought for a while, trying to put a face to the name. Finally, it gelled, and she smiled faintly, remembering the shock of wiry red hair, the freckled face and the man's shy, awkward manner.

'I remember him,' she said quietly. 'He was my first customer. He was quite nice.'

Ann waggled the phone impatiently. 'I don't care if he was Jack the bloody Ripper. Get over here fast. He's in a phone-box.'

The girl skipped across the room, snatching the phone. 'Hello, Ginger? Nice to hear from you again.' She paused, listening for a while before cupping her hand over the mouthpiece and hissing across to Ann. 'He wants me to meet him. Can I bring him back here?'

Ann Kirk's face registered annoyance. 'I'm hoping for a customer of my own tonight. You'll have to find somewhere else.'

Jenny spoke into the phone again. 'Look, I can meet you down by the river — on the embankment. About fifteen minutes, is that all right?'

She dropped the receiver back into its cradle and hurried to the mirror, hastily freshening her make-up. Dropping a few things into her handbag, she picked up her coat from the back of a chair and headed for the door.

She stopped suddenly, in mid-stride, as a thought struck her. 'Ginger,' she muttered aloud. 'Gingerbread Men.'

Ann looked at her over her shoulder. 'What?'

Jenny shook her head absently. 'Just something I remembered,' she said. 'Something the police asked me about.' She walked out of the door.

It was a cool night, with a chill breeze blowing off the river. Jenny huddled under a bridge, pulling her coat more tightly around her body, shivering slightly. It was not the sort of night to stand around in the open air, and she had already been waiting more than ten minutes. There was no sign of Ginger.

Jenny glanced at her watch. She would give him just another five minutes, she vowed, then she was going home. Her eyes strayed over to the light of a telephone box on the street corner, its yellow glow making it appear warm and inviting against the gloom and cold of the embankment. She thought of Taggart again, and his concern for 'Gingerbread Men'. Perhaps she should call him and tell him what she had remembered. Despite Ann's insistence that the police were their enemies, she could see no harm in helping them. And if it would help Jimmy Buchanan at the same time, then so much the better. He, too, had been an essentially kind man.

Jenny made up her mind. She walked towards the telephone box, fishing for some small change in her handbag. She entered the box and dialled directory enquiries.

'Hello, could you give me the number of Maryhill Police Station, please?'

Jenny scribbled the number down on the back of her hand with an eyebrow pencil. Finding a ten pence coin she placed it in the slot and dialled the number.

'I want to speak to Detective Taggart,' she said, as the duty sergeant answered the phone.

There was a longish pause. Finally, the duty sergeant spoke again, his voice apologetic. 'Sorry miss — Chief Inspector Taggart has gone home. I can let you speak to another officer if you like.'

Jenny racked her brains trying to think of the names of the other police officers. They escaped her completely. For a moment she nearly gave up and was about to replace the receiver.

She was vaguely aware of movement outside the telephone box, but ignored it, assuming it was someone else waiting to use the phone.

'Look, do you want to talk to another officer or not?' the duty sergeant at the station was asking.

'Okay — but it will have to be someone who knows about a missing guy called Jimmy Buchanan,' Jenny said. There was another long pause before the call was transferred.

'Hello, who is this?' came McVitie's voice eventually.

'My name's Jenny McClusky. I was interviewed by Chief Inspector Taggart yesterday and he asked me if "Gingerbread Men" meant anything.'

'Yes?' Mcvitie's voice was suddenly alert, urgent.

Jenny was not aware of the door of the telephone box being opened stealthily behind her. Nor of the hooded figure in a dark blue rain cape wielding a vicious cut-throat razor.

'I've only just remembered,' Jenny said. 'It's not Gingerbread Men at all. It's —'

McVitie heard only a choked and horrible scream after that, followed by several swishing, slicing noises and the sound of a brief, one-sided struggle.

'Hello . . . hello?' he shouted into the phone, but there was no answer.

For Jenny would never be able to tell him what he wanted

138

to know. She slid slowly down the blood-spattered glass of the telephone box, finally sitting in a crumpled heap on the floor like some life-sized puppet whose strings had just been cut.

Chapter Nineteen

Jardine leapt to his feet at the sound of the key in the lock. Like a love-sick puppy, he waited expectantly for Gemma to come in and make a fuss of him as she let herself into the flat.

If he had been expecting some sort of apology, it was not forthcoming. Gemma sauntered casually into the room and threw herself down on the sofa.

'Hi. What sort of an evening did you have?' she enquired politely.

Jardine frowned at her. 'Terrible,' he said. 'I was bored stiff. I was really looking forward to going to the Riverside Club tonight.'

Gemma shrugged carelessly. 'We can go another night. I really didn't have a choice, Mike. When your boss phoned so unexpectedly and said that he'd talk to me, I had to jump at the opportunity while I could. You know how important this book is to me.'

Jardine conceded the point grudgingly. 'Yes, I know,' he

muttered. 'It's just that Taggart seems to have a God-given talent for screwing up my life.'

'Actually, I think he rather respects you,' Gemma told him. 'I don't think he's quite the ogre you've made him out to be.'

Jardine grunted, unconvinced. 'That rather depends on where you're standing. Anyway — what made him change his mind?'

'Oh, I think he just wanted to correct a few facts, get some things straight.'

'What sort of things?'

Gemma was deliberately evasive. 'Little things — you know?'

'No, I don't know,' Jardine reminded her. 'And what are these "facts" he needed to correct?'

Gemma could see that her attempt at diplomacy was not going to work. 'Well, like who it was who came up with the contact lens clue in the Bowman case, for instance.'

Jardine opened his mouth to argue the point. Gemma rose from the sofa and quickly stepped in front of him. She pressed her finger gently over his lips.

'Mike, I've interviewed dozens of police officers over the years. They all have selective memories. Yours was just a little more selective than most.' She took her finger away, smiling.

Jardine looked like a little boy caught at the biscuit jar. 'I suppose he took the credit for everything,' he muttered, a trifle petulantly.

Gemma shook her head. 'No, not everything. In fact, he said that you were a very good foot soldier to his intuitive command.'

Jardine exploded with righteous indignation. 'He said *what*?'

Gemma grinned wickedly. 'I'm winding you up,' she admitted.

Despite himself, Jardine had to smile. He relaxed, leaning forward to kiss her. Gemma pulled him down on to the sofa beside her, their lips still locked together. It was a very long kiss, broken finally by the unwelcome sound of the telephone ringing.

Jardine's initial reaction was to ignore it.

'It could be important,' Gemma pointed out after a few seconds, pulling away from him.

'*You're* important,' Jardine murmured, trying to get back into a clinch, but the mood was broken. Jardine cursed under his breath, got to his feet and crossed to the telephone.

It was Taggart, of course. It *had* to be Taggart. Jardine listened as his superior filled him in with the basic details of Jenny McClusky's murder. Finally, he hung up the phone and started over towards Gemma in exasperation.

'You see? What was I just saying? That man is determined to screw up my life.'

'I take it you've got to go out?' Gemma said.

Jardine nodded. 'I don't know how long I'll be, but you'd better not wait up for me.'

Gemma flashed him a strange, almost affronted look. 'I wasn't planning to. Actually, I thought I'd work for an hour or so and then go to bed. Try not to wake me when you come in, there's a sweetie.'

Jardine frowned, aware that he had somehow said the wrong thing, but not quite sure what it was.

Whatever it had been, it was probably better left alone for now. He returned to the sofa, bent over and kissed Gemma lightly on the forehead. 'I'll see you in the morning,' he murmured, leaving it at that.

The body of Jenny McClusky lay on the mortuary slab, white, naked and horribly mutilated. Her blonde head lolled sideways at a loose, awkward angle from her shoulders, the muscles of her neck severed along with her blood vessels and windpipe. Caked, dried blood covered most of her face and upper torso.

'She was slashed five times with what appears to have been an open razor,' Dr Andrews informed Taggart and Jardine.

'Could it have been the same weapon that was used on Tom Barrow?' Taggart wanted to know.

Andrews nodded. 'That's a strong possibility,' he conceded. 'I can tell you that it was almost certainly wielded by the same person. The cuts are almost identical — right to left, same depth, same length.'

'Who was she phoning, do we know?' Jardine asked Taggart.

'She was phoning me,' McVitie said, coming up behind them. He touched Taggart lightly on the shoulder. 'She asked for you, Jim, but you'd gone home.'

'What did she want?'

'She said she had some information about Gingerbread.'

Taggart's ears pricked. 'What information?'

McVitie shook his head sadly. 'She never got a chance to tell me. Only that it was in connection with the disappearance of Jimmy Buchanan, and that we had it wrong. She was insistent about that. She said it was *not Gingerbread Men*.'

'Then what?' Taggart muttered, a perplexed look on his face.

McVitie shrugged hopelessly. 'Those were her last words.'

Jardine looked across at Taggart, sharing an expression of frustration. 'What now?'

'We'd better go and see her flatmate,' Taggart suggested. 'See if she knows anything.'

'Oh, Jim,' Dr Andrews said, just as he was about to leave. 'I managed to get a couple of prints off that hand. The thumb and one finger. They're not perfect, but they should be enough to get a match. Anyway, I sent a set off for computer enhancement, and they'll be back in the morning.'

The information brightened Taggart slightly. 'Thanks, Stephen. Good work.' He gave Jardine a grim smile. 'Well, maybe we're starting to get somewhere at last.'

Ann Kirk peered at them through the crack of the partly opened door, bleary-eyed and sour-looking. Devoid of her

143

harsh, tarty make-up, she appeared somehow prettier, less hard-looking.

Her voice and attitude, however, were unchanged. 'Oh, it's you bastards,' she spat out. 'Can't a girl get some sleep?'

'Jenny's getting plenty. In the mortuary,' Taggart said flatly.

The door sagged open. 'Aw, no.' There was a hopeless sob. 'You'd better come in.'

Ann opened the door fully and left them to close it behind them. She walked heavily across to the sofa and flopped down, seeming stunned.

'What happened?' she managed at last in a weak voice.

Taggart didn't answer her for the moment. 'Did she go out to meet a client tonight, or was she just streetwalking?' he wanted to know.

'She went to meet someone. It was someone she knew. She said he was all right, she'd been with him before.'

'Do you know who it was?' Jardine asked.

Ann nodded faintly. 'He called himself Ginger,' she said. 'But that probably wouldn't be his real name, of course.'

Taggart and Jardine exchanged a startled look. It seemed too damned close for coincidence.

'Did you know this guy?' Taggart asked hopefully.

Ann shook her head. 'I told you — *she* knew him, that's all. She said he was a nice guy.'

Jardine's face was grim with irony. 'There's a fair chance that this "nice" guy sliced her up with a razor,' he muttered.

Ann shuddered, the movement causing her dressing-gown to slide off one of her legs. Jardine noticed another long, ugly scar on her thigh.

'You'd know what that was like, Ann?' he said, not without sympathy.

The woman shrugged off his concern, suddenly sneering at him. 'You want to see the rest?' She pulled the dressing-gown away from her shoulder, exposing most of her left breast. It was a criss-cross patchwork of mutilating scars.

Jardine averted his eyes. Ann Kirk laughed bitterly at his

discomfiture, covering herself up again. 'No — of course you don't want to look. No one does.'

'Who did that to you?' Jardine asked.

Another short, savage explosion of mirthless laughter from Ann. 'How the hell should I know? I don't even remember what the bastard said his name was. I was drunk, seventeen and stupid. They had to pump so much blood into me none of it's my own.'

Things were digressing from the point, Taggart thought. 'Jenny rang us last night. She said she had some information about "Gingerbread Men". Do you know what that was?'

Ann shrugged. 'She muttered ginger-something just before she went out. I thought it was something to do with her client. I wasn't really listening.'

'So there's nothing you can tell us about this Ginger character?' Jardine said.

Ann thought for a few seconds, finally shaking her head. 'No. I'll ask around if you like. If I hear anything I'll let you know. Jenny was a good kid.'

'Aye, you do that,' Taggart grunted. He nodded across to Jardine, signalling that it was time to leave.

There was just one last thing, Jardine thought. 'What about Jenny's next of kin? Did she have anyone?'

'She had me,' Ann said. 'I never asked too many questions. All I know is that her parents are still in Ireland. She came over here for an abortion, like a lot of Irish girls.'

Jardine nodded, accepting the scant information. 'Okay, we'll trace her folks,' he promised. He turned to join Taggart, who was already heading for the door.

'Not much help, was she?" Jardine observed as the door closed behind them.

Taggart glanced at him with a faint look of surprise on his face. 'Did you expect there to be? She's hard, that one. She picked her side of the tracks, and we're on the other. We're the enemy, Michael. In her eyes, anyway.'

Jardine nodded. Taggart was right. The battle lines had been drawn up for a long time. 'So we can't really expect much help in tracking down this Ginger character?'

Taggart shrugged. 'Who knows? In the meantime, we start looking for ourselves. Tomorrow, I want you to start checking on all the massage parlours and known prostitutes in the area. It's quite likely he used the services of other girls.'

Jardine managed a faint smile. 'I didn't realise you knew so much about this side of the tracks, sir.'

The attempt at humour was not appreciated. Taggart glared at him briefly, but said nothing.

Chapter Twenty

Taggart was helping himself to a quick breakfast of toast and coffee as Jean wheeled herself into the kitchen, having been wakened by the smell of burning bread. She shooed him out of the way and popped a couple of fresh slices into the toaster.

'I didn't hear you come home last night,' she murmured conversationally.

Taggart sat himself down at the breakfast table. 'I was with a prostitute until four in the morning.'

The statement failed to make any impact. Jean Taggart was used to her husband's sometimes childish attempts to wind her up. 'I hope it was work,' she said casually.

Taggart sipped at his coffee. 'When is life anything else?'

The toaster pinged faintly. Jean took out the two perfectly browned slices of bread, buttered them, and put them on a plate. Wheeling herself up to the table, she put the toast down in front of him.

'I thought yesterday evening was a pleasant break for

you,' she observed. 'I haven't seen you in such a sociable mood for ages.' She paused briefly. 'Gemma seems a very nice young lady,' she added finally. 'Intelligent, too.'

Taggart crunched into his toast. 'Mike's very taken with her.'

Jean smiled to herself. 'I thought you rather overdid your part in some of those cases,' she pointed out to him.

Taggart bristled defensively. 'It's only for a book.'

'The kind of book you consider unhealthy,' Jean reminded him. 'The sort people only buy for a cheap thrill, and not because they're genuinely interested in real detective work.'

Taggart looked suitably chastened. 'Did I really say all that?' he asked, glancing across at her.

Jean nodded her head, a faint smile on her lips. 'Word for word. It's amazing how a pretty girl like Gemma can make you change your mind.'

Taggart attacked his toast again, a slightly sullen look on his face. 'That had nothing to do with it,' he muttered, knowing that she had him on the defensive and hating it.

He finished his breakfast in silence, finally draining his coffee cup and pushing himself to his feet.

'Will you be talking to prostitutes again tonight?' Jean asked half-jokingly, wanting to send him off to work on a more lighthearted note.

Taggart gave his wife a thin smile, appreciating what she was trying to do. 'I'll tell you one thing,' he said. 'I'd rather be talking to a murderer.'

Jardine was examining the contents of a small box for the umpteenth time when Taggart strode into the outer office on his way to see McVitie.

'Where were you earlier this morning?' he demanded gruffly. 'Things have been happening.'

Jardine hurriedly slipped the box into his pocket somewhat furtively. He looked up at Taggart, an embarrassed look on his face. 'Sorry, I was a bit late, sir. I had something I wanted to do.' He paused, trying to recover his composure. 'So, what developments?'

'Gault phoned me,' Taggart informed him. 'The prints we got off that hand check with those of Phillip Chalmers. So now we at least know that we're on the right track.'

Jardine digested the information. 'That is good news — at last.'

Taggart merely nodded. 'Anyway, The Biscuit wants to see us both,' he said, using McVitie's common nickname. 'Are you coming? Or have you something else you want to do?'

Jardine was still obviously flustered. He fumbled with some papers on his desk, shuffling them around looking for his notebook. Remembering it was in his pocket, he pulled it out. Several other slips of paper came out at the same time. Jardine scooped them up and pushed them into a little pile on his desk.

Finally, he got to his feet.

'Are you with us at last?' Taggart enquired sarcastically. Without waiting for an answer he led the way to McVitie's office.

'It seems to me that we have three priorities,' McVitie said after they had both sat down. 'Firstly, we find the rest of Phillip Chalmers' body.'

Taggart interrupted him. 'We're waiting for the dog to do that, sir.'

McVitie frowned at him briefly. 'Secondly, we find this Ginger and then, hopefully, we learn the meaning of what Jenny McClusky was trying to tell us before she was killed,' he concluded.

'There must be a lot of people called Ginger in Glasgow, sir,' Jardine put in, slightly indignant. McVitie had managed to make it sound as though it was a simple, five-minute job.

McVitie conceded the point grudgingly. 'I think it's fairly safe to assume that he's red-haired, for a start. He looked directly at Taggart. 'Where will you be directing your investigations?'

'I think it's probable that he's been to other prostitutes in

Glasgow,' Taggart answered him. 'We'll start looking there.'

McVitie nodded thoughtfully. 'That seems sensible. Now, has anyone any ideas on what Jenny might have meant when she said "*not* Gingerbread Men"?'

Taggart shook his head. 'All I know, sir, is that Tom Barrow was killed because he found out something about Phillip Chalmers' murder. Jenny, obviously, for the same reason, although what the connection is I have no idea at the moment.'

The frank admission seemed to bring the briefing to a natural conclusion. Taggart stood up. 'If anyone asks where I am, I'll be in Edinburgh seeing Mrs Chalmers.'

'What do you want me to do, sir?' Jardine asked. 'It's a bit early in the day to start touring the red light district.'

Taggart thought for a moment. 'I suppose you could always pop round and find out how Operation Walkies is going,' he suggested.

Not very well, would have been Jackie Reid's answer. The dog had steadfastly refused to leave the house all night, with the stubbornness of his species. It now hovered around the breakfast table in Dave Jobson's kitchen, its tail wagging expectantly.

Jobson cut one of his sausages in half, holding it down to the animal, who wolfed it down greedily.

'I do wish you'd stop doing that,' Jackie snapped, her patience sorely tried by the sheer boredom of the whole operation.

Jobson looked up at her, startled by the vehemence in her tone.

'I mean, we want him to wander off, don't we?' Jackie went on. 'He's hardly likely to go foraging with a three-course breakfast in his belly. We could be here until Christmas.'

Jobson looked pained. 'You mean starve him? Starve my dog?'

'Just for a day, at least,' Jackie said, adopting a more conciliatory tone. 'Please!'

Jobson reached down to pat the animal's head. 'Do you hear that, Rusty? The Strathclyde Police don't want you to have any breakfast.'

Wynn-Davies peered over the top of the paper he had been reading. 'Actually, it's a well-documented fact that dogs can survive for up to two months without food,' he announced.

Jackie gave him an exasperated look. 'Actually, it's another well-known fact that if I'm stuck here with you two for much longer I'll go spare,' she said cuttingly.

Jardine's arrival came as a welcome break. He sat down at the table with Jobson and Wynn-Davies as Jackie got up to make him a cup of tea. Absently, he picked up a piece of uneaten toast and broke a piece off, feeding it to the dog just as Jackie turned round with his tea in her hand.

'Not you as well!' she screamed out in frustration. 'Now I've got another cloth-brained male to contend with.'

Jardine looked up in surprise, not sure what he'd done wrong.

'I don't know how you manage to work with her,' Jobson observed morosely. 'She's been like that for the past twenty-four hours.'

Jackie slammed Jardine's teacup down on the table. 'We're trying to starve the mutt,' she explained, spelling it out. 'We want him to go a-wandering, don't we?'

Jardine looked apologetic. 'Sorry, I wasn't thinking,' he murmured.

Jackie regarded him curiously. 'Have you got something on your mind?' she asked.

Jardine looked relieved. He smiled at her secretively. 'Actually, I want to show you something,' he confided. He nodded his head in the direction of the door, rising to his feet.

Jackie followed him out into the garden, intrigued. 'So, what's the big secret?'

Jardine fished in his pocket and pulled out the small box

which had obsessed his thoughts for most of the morning. Thumbing open the hinged lid, he displayed its contents for Jackie's approval.

She regarded the diamond and sapphire engagement ring with enthusiasm. 'Mike, it's gorgeous,' she breathed. 'It must have set you back a small fortune.'

Jardine shrugged off his extravagance with a gesture of male nonchalance. 'I'm going to ask her tonight,' he confided. 'So don't say anything to anyone.'

Jackie's look of enthusiasm was clouded by the faintest show of concern. 'You're supposed to ask the girl first — and *then* buy the ring,' she pointed out.

Jardine looked a bit sheepish. 'I thought this way was more romantic,' he said.

Jackie glanced up briefly to see the childlike sparkle in his eyes. Her concern grew. He looked like a kid with a brand-new toy. But this was not kids' stuff. This was very much into grown-ups' territory, and Jardine seemed suddenly naïve and very vulnerable.

'Mike, you've only known her for a week and a half,' she felt obliged to point out, sounding a note of caution.

Jardine shook his head in denial, a dreamy smile on his face. 'I've known her sixteen years. It's like we've never been apart.'

Nothing could dampen his enthusiasm. Nor, perhaps, should it, Jackie thought. 'Well, you know what I mean,' she murmured lamely.

'Do you think she'll like it?' Jardine asked.

On that point Jackie could give her wholehearted approval. 'Mike, any woman would be thrilled to receive it,' she promised him.

With a proud smile Jardine closed the lid of the box and slipped it back into his pocket. He turned back towards the house just as Wynn-Davies came rushing out into the garden.

'Have you seen the dog?' he called to both of them. 'Did he come past you in the last couple of minutes?'

Jackie and Jardine exchanged a quick double-take. They

both exploded into action simultaneously, sprinting back towards the house.

'He didn't come past us,' Jackie said to Wynn-Davies as they ran back into the kitchen. 'The last time I saw him he was mooching around in here.'

'Well, he's not here now,' Wynn-Davies announced firmly. 'He's gone.'

Jackie glanced at the breakfast table, noting the empty plate where she had been sitting. The moment of hopeful optimism passed. 'So's the rest of my breakfast,' she observed with a sinking feeling. She walked slowly into the lounge and peered behind the back of the settee.

The dog looked up at her, its tail wagging furiously as it finished off the last of her breakfast sausages.

Chapter Twenty-one

'I suppose there's no doubt at all?' Elsa Chalmers asked.

Taggart shook his head. 'I'm sorry, Mrs Chalmers. We compared the computer enhanced prints with a set taken from your husband's electric shaver. There were enough points of similarity for us to be absolutely certain.'

Gault stepped forward and placed his arm gently around Elsa's shoulders, hugging her comfortingly. 'At least we know now, Elsa. All the waiting and uncertainty are over.'

'Yes, I suppose so.' Elsa seemed to take some solace from this. She was silent for a while, finally looking across at Taggart with a slightly resigned expression on her face. 'Where's the rest of him?'

Taggart's face was impassive. He could hardly tell her that they were waiting for a dog to dig up the rest of her husband's body. 'We're hoping we'll know that soon,' he said simply.

Elsa Chalmers bit at her lower lip, her composure cracking slightly. 'Poor Phillip. He didn't deserve this,' she said in a tight little voice.

Gault pulled out his cigarette case, offering it to Elsa. She shook her head. Gault helped himself to a yellow cigarette and lit it. 'There was another murder last night, Elsa,' he said quietly.

' A Glasgow prostitute,' Taggart filled in for him. 'She was killed by the same person who murdered the private detective you hired.'

Elsa seemed bemused by it all. 'Why?' she asked.

Taggart looked grim. 'That's what we have to find out. What the connection is.' He was thoughtful for a moment. 'Look, I know this is a highly personal and embarrassing question for you — but did your husband have any involvement with prostitutes?'

Elsa didn't answer him. Instead, she turned nervously to Gault. 'Bobby, could I have that cigarette now, please?'

With a slightly puzzled look, Gault pulled out a cigarette and handed it to her. He tried to light it for her, but Elsa's fingers were trembling violently. He looked across at Taggart. 'Look, could you leave us alone for a few minutes?' There was a mute plea in his eyes which Taggart chose to ignore.

Elsa fought to control herself, pulling Gault's wrist across and lighting her cigarette from the flaming lighter in his hand. She took a deep drag, sucked the smoke into her lungs and held it there for several seconds before exhaling.

'That won't be necessary,' she murmured, turning back to Taggart. She took a deep breath before continuing. 'Phillip preferred to refer to them as escorts,' she said calmly after a while. 'I found a list of names and telephone numbers in his briefcase once. Glasgow, Edinburgh, London. Girls, agencies, hotel contact points.'

'I don't suppose you've still got this list?' Taggart asked optimistically, knowing that it was probably too much to hope for.

Elsa shook her head, confirming his worst fears. 'I burnt it.'

'How long ago was this?' Gault asked.

'About two years ago. But there have been others since, I know.'

Taggart gaped at her, open-mouthed. 'You've known that your husband frequented prostitutes for two years?'

Elsa avoided his eyes, her expression shame-faced and penitent. She glanced up at Gault, who looked shocked. Taggart felt almost sorry for him.

'There wasn't much else I could do but try to ignore it,' Elsa muttered in a small, tight voice. 'It was a matter of keeping up appearances, you see. Putting on a respectable front.'

Taggart blew out through his teeth in a gesture of exasperation. This was Edinburgh gentility at its most hypocritical. He knew he should be angry, but he couldn't quite bring himself to express it. 'Mrs Chalmers — if we'd known about this eleven days ago . . .' The sentence tailed off into a sigh of resignation.

Elsa looked down at the floor. 'Call it my pride, I suppose.'

'Pride?' Taggart spat out. 'But you told Tom Barrow, didn't you?'

Elsa nodded faintly. 'I had to.'

'So why couldn't you bring yourself to tell us?' Taggart demanded.

'Because she didn't want me to find out,' Gault put in. He moved protectively between Taggart and Elsa like a human shield.

It was also a gesture of solidarity, of support, for Elsa's benefit. She accepted it gratefully, leaning her head against his shoulder.

'How could I tell you? What sort of wife would you have thought I was, who would let her husband go with prostitutes?'

Taggart glared at them both with undisguised contempt. He was heartily sick of the pair of them and their delicate little secrets. 'Between the two of you, your respectability and pride has caused us to waste eleven days of a murder inquiry.'

Gault's sense of guilt showed in his eyes. 'Surely it was understandable?' he muttered defensively.

Taggart's rage finally exploded. 'Understandable? I've got two corpses in the Glasgow mortuary. All in all, I don't give a damn for your precious little personal feelings.'

His anger dissipated into mere frustration. Taggart turned away in disgust, storming towards the door.

Gault put his arms around Elsa, hugging her. 'Look, Elsa — it will be all right. But I have to go now, you understand?'

Elsa nodded. 'I'm sorry, Bobby.'

'I'll come back just as soon as I can,' Gault promised her. With a final reassuring squeeze, he detached himself and set off after Taggart.

Taggart was waiting by his car, his face sullen. 'She could have saved us a lot of time,' he grumbled.

Gault was anxious to get back to business as usual. 'I'll handle all the escort agencies and massage parlours at this end,' he announced briskly.

Taggart couldn't resist a last sarcastic dig at the man. 'I didn't think you had such things in respectable Edinburgh.'

'They call them VIP services here,' Gault informed him with a straight face.

'Aye, they would,' Taggart grunted, opening the door of his car.

It was difficult to decide which was the most terminally boring — hanging around the house watching Jobson and Wynn-Davies glued to the football match on television or wandering around in the back garden watching the dog trot about aimlessly. Jackie Reid had chosen the garden, mainly because the dog was slightly more animated than its master and infinitely more interesting than Nigel Wynn-Davies.

The animal still showed no signs of taking off for the great outdoors. Apparently satisfied with its stolen breakfast, it seemed content to pace the confines of its home turf, occasionally pausing to sniff at a patch of turned earth, or the base of an uprooted shrub. No great animal lover at the best of times, Jackie had seriously considered applying the toe of her shoe to the animal's most sensitive parts more than once, but had so far resisted the temptation.

A shout from inside the house distracted her attention for a moment. Thankful for even the slightest break in routine, she moved towards the house to investigate. It turned out to be nothing more than a missed penalty kick. When Jackie returned to the garden the dog was gone.

She rushed back inside the house. 'He's gone!' she announced, the faintest trace of panic in her voice. After all the waiting, the possibility of losing the animal now was too terrible to contemplate.

Jobson continued to stare at the TV set. 'Oh, he's around somewhere,' he muttered carelessly.

Jackie regarded Wynn-Davies in disbelief. Sprawled full-length on the settee, he showed no sign of interest in the dog's whereabouts. 'This time he's gone, I tell you,' Jackie shouted. Choosing the only way she could think of to attract the man's attention, she strode across to the television and switched it off.

'Hadn't we better get after him?' she demanded.

Wynn-Davies uncoiled himself casually from the settee. 'No need to panic. I told you, we can track him from miles away.' He stooped down to pick up his portable monitor and switched it on. The instrument began to emit a regular bleeping noise. 'There, see what I mean? The computer equipment in the van will give us an exact fix on him.'

Not totally convinced, Jackie followed him out through the front of the house towards the surveillance van. They climbed in and Wynn-Davies switched on the computer, punching in the area co-ordinates. A map of the immediate area flashed up on the screen, with a small white blip marking the dog's position.

'There he is,' Wynn-Davies announced proudly. 'Looks like he's heading north-north-west across the gardens of that housing estate. Being a dog, of course, he won't necessarily travel by road.'

Jackie was not impressed by this earth-shaking revelation.

'Did you by any chance take a degree in animal behaviour?' she enquired sarcastically.

Wynn-Davies chose to ignore the remark. He started the engine up and slipped the van into gear, moving off down the street. At the first intersection he stopped, checking the dog's position on the computer screen once again.

'Oh, hang about — he's changing direction. Perhaps we should have brought in the helicopter as well.'

Jackie groaned aloud. 'Now you tell me,' she complained.

Wynn-Davies executed a three-point turn in the road and studied the screen again. 'No, it might be all right. We can still approach him at a tangent. It looks as though he's heading for open countryside, but don't worry. This vehicle will go almost anywhere.'

'So can a bloody dog,' Jackie pointed out with heavy emphasis. With a slight sinking feeling, she watched the small blip on the screen moving further and further away from the van's position.

Betty Duncan proudly put the finishing touches to the gingerbread house she had made with such loving care. It was an intricate and detailed confection, with the sloping roof thatched with chocolate strands and finished off with touches of frosted icing to simulate snow. There were even tiny window-boxes complete with miniature flowers crafted from marzipan and rice paper. Betty carefully arranged the three human figures she had moulded into a tableau outside the chocolate door. The small, delicate Gretel, the slightly larger figure of her brother Hansel — and the bent, evil body of the witch in her pointed hat.

She stepped back to admire her work, pleased with herself. Her husband would have been proud of her, she thought. Now, if only the children would come again, everything would be all right.

There was a loud knocking on the back door. With a little surge of excitement, Betty moved quickly to answer it throwing the door open with a beaming, welcoming smile on her face. It faded slightly as she recognised Joe Soutar.

'Oh, it's you, Joe?'

Soutar grinned. 'Why, were you expecting visitors?' he asked. He jerked his thumb out towards his van and trailer, piled high with freshly cut logs. 'I brought you some logs — cut nice and small, as you like them.'

'Thank you, Joe,' Betty murmured. She stood in the doorway uncertainly.

'Any chance of a cup of tea?' the man prompted, realising that she wasn't going to offer. 'The thing is, the van's playing up and overheating, and I need to let the engine cool down for a while.'

Betty backed into the cottage awkwardly. 'Yes, of course — sorry.'

Soutar stepped over the threshold, his eyes falling on the immaculate gingerbread house. 'So you *are* expecting visitors,' he observed.

'Just the children. Simon and his sister. I thought they might come again,' Betty said.

Soutar seated himself at the table. 'I saw the boy the other day,' he told her. 'Seems you shut the door on him. He was quite upset.'

Betty's face clouded over. 'He came uninvited,' she said. 'He surprised me, that's all. I didn't mean to upset him.'

She crossed to the food cupboard and brought out a plate of gingerbread men, setting it down on the table in front of Soutar. 'Help yourself,' she said. 'I'll just make a fresh pot of tea.'

Soutar picked up a gingerbread man and bit its head off, savouring the rich, spicy taste. 'Wish I had a ma like you, Betty,' he mumbled appreciatively.

Betty turned away to the Aga, lifting the ever-boiling kettle and pouring it into the teapot to scald it. Soutar glanced at the collection of photographs on the sideboard, noting one of a much younger Betty surrounded by her three children.

'What about your own kids, Betty? Do they ever come to see you now?'

Betty looked round at him, a slightly startled look on her face. 'No, never.'

'But you get quite a lot of visitors,' Soutar pointed out. 'I've seen them. I always thought they were your family.'

He returned his eyes to the table, biting into his gingerbread man again, unaware that Betty had frozen in the act of making the tea, and was now glaring at him with fear and suspicion in her eyes.

Chapter Twenty-two

Wynn-Davies pulled the surveillance van to a halt by the side of the road. They were out into open countryside now, surrounded by woodland.

'I think we're going to have to get out and follow him on foot now,' Wynn-Davies announced, switching off the engine.

Jackie glanced sideways at him, a concerned look on her face. 'I thought you said this van could go anywhere?'

'Not through trees, it can't,' Wynn-Davies said, pointing ahead to a patch of dense woodland. 'He's in there, and making a bee-line for whatever it is he's after.' He threw the portable monitor over his shoulder and climbed out of the van.

Jackie jumped out to join him, skirting around the front of the vehicle. 'We'd better get moving, then.'

Wynn-Davies consulted his monitor. 'No hurry,' he murmured. 'He's stopped. It seems he's found what he was looking for.' He made no attempt to move.

'Well, don't you think we should go and check it out?' Jackie asked.

Wynn-Davies looked cautious. 'We don't want to alert him to our presence.'

Jackie flashed him a scathing look. 'He's a bloody dog, not a terrorist,' she reminded him. She patted him on the arm. 'Come on, let's go and see what he's up to.'

Reluctantly, Wynn-Davies followed her as she began to walk towards the woods, scrambling up a steep, grassy bank. 'I've got my good trousers on,' he complained, hesitating.

Jackie stopped and looked back down at him, infuriated. 'So what do you do when you corner an armed suspect with a hostage? Nip home and change?' she demanded. 'Now, come on — and stop whingeing.'

Muttering something under his breath Wynn-Davies began to clamber up the bank behind her. Reaching the top, Jackie plunged into the dense undergrowth and began to push her way through it.

They finally came in sight of a small clearing. Treading warily, Jackie picked her way through the last clump of brambles and peered into the open space. All the frustration of the past couple of days finally came to a head and was let out in a single, explosive scream.

Wynn-Davies hurried to join her, alarm on his face. He too stared into the clearing, following her point of view.

The dog was there all right, but not alone. It had, in fact, found exactly what it was seeking. As Wynn-Davies and Jackie watched, it humped itself up over the back of a large Labrador bitch and began copulating furiously.

Wynn-Davies, at least, could see the funny side of it. He laughed, turning aside to Jackie. 'I think he's in love,' he observed.

She was not amused. 'Like somebody else I know,' she muttered darkly.

The man in question was at that moment seated in a pub with Taggart, grabbing a quick pie and a pint for lunch.

Taggart slid a photograph across the table. 'Here's a picture of Phillip Chalmers,' he said. 'You'll need it — only don't forget that he probably didn't use his real name.'

Jardine picked up the photograph, studying it carefully. Phillip Chalmers was, or had been, a suave, handsome man.

'It doesn't make sense, does it?' he asked Taggart. 'Here's a man with plenty of money, good looks and all the right social connections. Why should he want to use the services of prostitutes?'

Taggart shrugged. There wasn't really a good answer to that one. 'People do strange things, Michael.'

Jardine frowned thoughtfully. 'Can't Mrs Chalmers remember a single name on that list?' he asked. 'Something which would at least give us a starting point?'

Taggart shook his head. 'She just blotted it out,' he said. 'And I don't suppose I can blame her.'

'So we start from scratch? All the massage parlours, all the "escort" agencies which advertise in the papers and all the 0898 telephone lines that masquerade as matchmaker services.'

Taggart nodded. 'And don't forget to carry plenty of ten pence pieces with you,' he pointed out. 'Those dating lines are usually just recorded messages with a list of other phone numbers right at the end.' He broke off, sighing. 'I must admit, it was all a lot simpler in my day. Ten bob for a tart and straight up the back alley.'

He extended his hand across the table. 'Congratulations, by the way.'

Jardine looked at him suspiciously. 'For what?'

'Gemma's a nice girl,' Taggart said. 'I hope she likes that ring you've got in your pocket.'

Jardine's face fell. 'How did you know about that?'

Taggart grinned. 'You were in such a fluster in the office, you left the receipt on the top of your desk. I think we must be paying you too much.'

Jardine smiled ruefully. He reached across the table and accepted his chief's proffered handshake. 'Actually, I haven't asked her yet,' he confessed.

'Well, get this job done before you do,' Taggart suggested. 'We've wasted enough time as it is.'

From his hiding place amongst the trees, Simon watched Joe Soutar come out of the rear door of Betty Duncan's cottage and climb into his van. The engine coughed, black smoke belching from the exhaust. Simon stayed concealed as the van jerked heavily away down the lane towards the main road, pondering his next move.

He really didn't have a plan at all, Simon realised. In fact, he wasn't even sure at that moment why he had come to the cottage at all. Certainly not to confront the old woman, who would surely just send him packing again. As he waited, wondering, fate took its own hand in things.

Simon ducked further back into the cover of the trees as the front door of the cottage opened and Betty stepped out, a large earthenware bowl in her hands. She walked away from the house, deep into the surrounding bushes and began to pick blackberries.

Simon acted on impulse. Taking advantage of Betty's turned back, he crept out from his hiding place and began to run towards the back door of the cottage. As he had expected, it was unlocked. Stealthily, Simon let himself into the kitchen, his heart pounding in his chest.

He stared at the gingerbread house in amazement. Looking closer, he examined the little figures of the boy, the girl and the witch. Oddly, he found himself comparing them to himself and Nicola, and a passage from *Hansel and Gretel* sprang unbidden into his mind.

The old woman only pretended to be so kind: she was in reality a wicked witch, who lay in wait for children, and had only built the little house of bread in order to entice them there . . .

Simon shrugged the thoughts from his mind, tearing his eyes away from the gingerbread house. He moved towards the stairs and began to creep up them slowly towards the locked door on the landing.

It was still locked he discovered, as he tried the handle. Frustrated, he was about to creep away again when he heard the unmistakable sounds of movement from inside the room.

Simon's stomach turned to ice and a lump formed in his throat. With a sudden shiver of fear, he turned away from the door and began to run down the stairs two at a time, bolting out of the back door.

Running blindly across the yard, he cannoned headlong into Betty, who was just returning from her fruit-picking. The bowl of blackberries went flying. A surprisingly strong pair of hands seized him roughly by the shoulders.

Betty Duncan's face was contorted with rage as she shook him violently. 'What are you doing here?' she hissed. 'You've been spying on me, haven't you?'

Simon could only shake his head, trying to mouth a denial. But words refused to come to his lips.

Betty shook him again, like a rag doll. 'The first time I thought it was because you were hungry — but now I know. You came to pry, to steal into my house and meddle in things which don't concern you.'

Simon found his voice at last. 'Let me go! You're hurting me,' he cried, but it was no use. The woman continued to hold him in a vice-like grip.

'Who are you? What do you want?' she demanded, her voice harsh and grating.

Simon ceased struggling. He looked up at her with defiant eyes, his desperate need lending him sudden strength. 'I want to know who killed my father.'

The effect of the words was immediate and dramatic.

Betty pushed him away from her, as though she had suddenly realised that she was holding something indescribably repulsive. She took a couple of steps backwards, regarding him with a look of shock and horror on her hag-like face.

'Go! Go away from here at once,' she shouted at him.

'Get away from this place and never, never come back, do you hear?'

Simon needed no second bidding. Relieved to be free, he turned on his heels and sprinted away into the woods.

Betty Duncan stood watching his departing figure until he had disappeared into the trees. Slowly she turned towards the house, and her eyes strayed to the upstairs window. Her body shuddered convulsively as a racking sob tore through her.

When she finally tore her eyes away, they were moist with tears.

Chapter Twenty-three

'So, Operation Walkies wasn't exactly what you would call your greatest success?' Jardine said.

Jackie Reid regarded him with a sour expression. 'Give me criminals any day. At least they're predictable. But dogs — forget them.'

She stared moodily ahead, down the gloomy and sordid back-streets of the city's red light district. 'Mind you, I don't think I've exactly made an upwards career move.'

'Welcome back to the real world,' Jardine said.

They had just come to yet another basement massage parlour, its presence announced by a tacky red neon sign sticking out of a bare brick wall.

'This is the real world?' Jackie queried. She gazed down an unlit flight of iron steps which led to a plain wooden door. 'I suppose we do have to go in there?'

Jardine nodded. 'Look on the bright side — this is the last one. After that we move to the sophisticated end of the market.'

'After you,' Jackie said graciously. She stood back as Jardine started to descend the steps, then followed him down.

An overpowering smell of cheap make-up, stale sweat and massage oil assaulted their nostrils as Jardine pushed open the door. The tiny reception area was at least reasonably clean, and staffed by a garishly made-up woman in her middle forties who sat behind a small desk. She looked up with only a flicker of interest as Jardine and Jackie walked in.

'Into kinky double acts, are we, love?' she enquired of Jardine. 'Not sure we can accommodate you. This is a respectable establishment.'

Jardine smiled. 'Yeah, and I'm Mary Whitehouse's right-hand man.' He flashed his police ID card, watching the woman's face. It showed the faintest trace of concern. 'Relax, we're not the Vice Squad,' he told her.

The woman stared at them with open contempt, a mocking smile on her heavily painted lips. 'No skin off my nose if you were, love. There's no vice here.'

As if to negate this statement, a topless and busty blonde suddenly popped out from behind a curtained cubicle. She started to smile at Jardine, but a quick glare from the manageress froze her in her tracks. Wordlessly, she swivelled on her heels and disappeared back behind the curtain.

'We're making enquiries about two people who might be clients,' Jardine said. 'This is one of them.' He passed the photograph of Phillip Chalmers across the counter. 'His name's Phillip Chalmers, but he may not have used that name.'

The woman gave the picture only a fleeting, disinterested glance before passing it back. 'Never seen him, don't know the name. I told that to the other detective.'

Jackie Reid's ears pricked. 'Was his name Barrow, by any chance?'

The manageress shrugged. 'Something like that.'

'When did he come in here?' Jardine wanted to know.

The woman threw a cursory glance at a calendar on the wall. 'About ten days ago.'

'He was murdered ten days ago,' Reid put in.

The woman's face was emotionless. 'Yeah, I read something about that,' she said casually.

'Of course, it wouldn't have occurred to you to come forward with this information?' Jackie asked sarcastically.

'I've got a business to run, love.' The woman stuck a cigarette between her lips and lit it, blowing a plume of smoke directly into Jackie's face.

Jardine couldn't take any more. He stepped forward, snatched the cigarette out of the woman's mouth and ground it out in the ashtray.

'We've got a business to run, too,' he snapped. 'We're also looking for someone who might call himself Ginger.'

The manageress remained unimpressed by the strong-arm tactics. She glared at Jardine with open defiance. 'Got red hair, has he?'

Jardine walked right into it. 'Yes, he could have.'

'Sorry, don't know anyone of that name or description.' She sneered at Jardine. 'Not your lucky night, love, is it?'

Jackie tried one more approach to the woman's better nature, if she had one. 'Look, this "Ginger" might be responsible for the savage murder of a prostitute last night. Don't you care?'

A careless shrug gave her the answer. 'Shouldn't be on the streets, should they?' the woman said callously.

Jackie grabbed Jardine's arm, pulling him away. 'Come on, we're not going to get anything here. Let's try that sophisticated end of the market you were talking about.'

They returned outside to the streets. Jackie breathed deeply, sucking the cool night air into her lungs. 'Good to get a breath of fresh air, isn't it?'

Jardine nodded, knowing that she meant it in more ways than one. 'Come on, let's get back to the car. Now we start on the telephone dating services.'

Billy Jackson sat at a desk in his grubby little flat, surrounded by card index files and multi-line telephone answering tape-decks. The phone rang at the same time as he heard the knock on his door.

Business came first. Billy picked up the phone. 'Strathclyde Dateline Escort Express. How can I help you?' He rifled through one of the card index files as the caller gave him a reference number. 'E26 — that's Lucinda, a real cracker. After the tone, listen carefully for her exclusive private telephone number. Your pleasure is my pleasure. Call again.'

There was a second, more insistent knock at the door. Billy flicked the answering machine on to automatic and rose to his feet.

Billy recognised his caller as he opened the door. 'Well, well, well. Sergeant Jardine. Long time no see,' he muttered, the shifty smile on his face belying the tone of his voice.

'Not long enough, Billy,' Jardine snapped, walking in and taking a quick look around. 'Well, fancy finding you at this game. Bottom fallen out of the porn video market, has it?'

Jackie was taking a good look around the filthy flat. She turned over a small pile of dirty socks and underpants with her foot, exposing a couple of pornographic magazines underneath. 'This is the sophisticated end?' she muttered with heavy irony.

'This is legitimate,' Billy said. He sounded almost proud of his little business empire. 'Rented a line from BT, all highly respectable. Dating services for the shy and lonely.'

'Who pay fifty pence a minute for your recorded messages,' Jackie pointed out.

Billy was unconcerned. 'That's peak rate. All strictly legal.'

'Peak rip-off, more like,' Jackie retorted.

Billy grinned at her. 'Telecommunications is big business. Where the money is.' He looked across at Jardine. 'So, what can I do for you?'

Jardine faced him squarely. 'This is a murder inquiry, Billy,' he muttered.

The man shrugged carelessly. 'Not guilty. Now, can I get back to work?'

'Just as soon as you answer a few questions,' Jardine told him. 'A client calling himself Ginger. Ring any bells?'

The ingratiating smile faded from Billy's face, to be replaced by a shifty, evasive expression. 'Look, Sergeant Jardine — I get hundreds of calls every night, mostly from Jimmys. They give me the reference numbers of girls they've heard on the tape and I give them the telephone numbers. That's all.'

'So you'd remember a Ginger?' Jackie stressed.

Billy looked uncertain. 'All right, there is a guy called Ginger who uses us quite a lot,' he said, after a while. 'He called earlier tonight, as a matter of fact.'

Jardine jumped on this information. 'Who was he going to see?'

'A girl called Tina — Afro-Asian chick,' Billy told him, somewhat reluctantly. 'I told him she was busy until nine o'clock.'

Jardine glanced at his watch hurriedly. It was 8.45. He grabbed a piece of paper and a pen from Billy's desk, thrusting it under the man's nose. 'Her full name and address — now,' he barked.

Billy took the paper and began to scribble down the details. He handed it back to Jardine with a grin. 'You know, you're beginning to develop your boss's manners,' he observed.

Jardine let the remark pass. There was no time for further small talk. He turned to Jackie, his voice urgent. 'Right, let's go. With a bit of luck we can get there before him. We'll call Taggart from the car.'

'Don't tell me. You have to go out again tonight,' Jean Taggart said resignedly, as Taggart hung up the phone.

Taggart retrieved his tie from the back of his easy chair and started to put it on. 'Could be important. Ginger's on his way to a flat in Anniesland.'

'How do you know it's the same Ginger?' his wife asked.

'I don't. We just hope.' He finished knotting his tie and

172

leaned over to kiss Jean on the forehead. 'Oh, by the way —
Mike's getting engaged to Gemma tonight. Romantic, isn't
it?'

'Well, I just hope he's more romantic about than you
were,' Jean said, smiling. 'You proposed to me in a bus shel-
ter.'

Taggart slipped on his jacket. 'Yes, well — it was raining,
wasn't it?' He made his exit before Jean could reply.

Chapter Twenty-four

Willie Frazer paced up and down the room nervously, glancing at his watch every five or six seconds.

Brockwell relaxed on the sofa, a calm, philosophical smile on his face. 'Why don't you relax? I'm sure Simon is all right.'

Frazer consulted his watch again. 'But it's nearly nine o'clock. He's never run off for this long before.'

'Look, he's a sensible boy,' Brockwell pointed out. 'I'm sure he wouldn't just have run away. He'll be back soon, I'm sure of it.'

'Things still happen to sensible boys,' Jessie Frazer put in. 'Especially with the number of wicked people out there.'

Brockwell turned his attention to his sister. 'Simon wouldn't go off with any strangers,' he assured her.

Jessie was not convinced. 'Sometimes it's not the strangers you have to worry about.'

She broke off suddenly, listening intently. 'What's that?'

Brockwell shook his head. 'I didn't hear anything.'

Jessie was already moving towards the living-room door.

'I thought I heard the front door opening.' She pulled the door open, catching Simon in the act of starting to creep up the stairs. Caught in the act, he froze in his tracks like a startled rabbit, regarding her with a guilty look on his face.

Behind her, Willie Frazer's earlier tension and worry found release in anger. He pushed past his wife, confronting the boy.

'Where have you been?' he demanded harshly. 'Don't you know what time it is?'

Simon said nothing, merely glaring at them both with a sullen look on his face.

'We worry about you,' Jessie Frazer said in a gentler tone.

Simon shook his head. 'No, you don't,' he shot back. 'You don't care — nobody cares.'

Ever the mediator, Brockwell put in his own contribution. 'Of course we worry about you, Simon — as though we were your family.'

'And as long as you live in this house, young man, we are your family and you'll come home at a reasonable hour,' Frazer added.

It was the wrong thing to say. Simon turned back to the door, shouting at them all in defiance. 'You're *not* my family — any of you. And I don't need you.'

With that he was out of the door again, slamming it behind him. He ran off into the night, confused, insecure and unsure of why he was running, let alone where.

Frazer started to go after him, but Brockwell laid a restraining hand on his shoulder. 'We'd better telephone Sergeant Jardine,' he muttered softly.

'Ginger' McGarrity paused under a street-light to check the address he had scribbled down on a slip of paper, consulting his watch at the same time. It was 9.05 and he was on the right street. He glanced up at the row of terraced houses, trying to pick out the numbers. Identifying the house he wanted, he pulled a comb from the pocket of his anorak and ran it through his shock of wiry red hair. It didn't make a great deal of difference, other than to give him a psychological boost of confidence. He'd heard stories about Afro-Asian women. They were supposed to be hot stuff, but they were fussy about personal appearance. Ginger grinned to himself. Well, *he* was feeling hot stuff tonight, and he'd give this Tina a real good seeing to.

Yes indeed! A real good seeing to.

Feeling pleased with himself, he walked briskly towards the apartment house and up the flight of stone steps to the front door. He surveyed a veritable keyboard of bells and name-plates, vaguely aware of someone coming up the steps behind him.

The fact in itself was no cause for alarm. There must be at least twenty flats and bedsits in the house. Obviously, there would be a lot of two-way traffic. Ginger finally identified Tina's bell and pushed it.

A strong hand gripped his elbow. 'Is your name Ginger?' a gruff voice demanded.

Ginger's head whipped sideways, to be confronted by Taggart's grim face.

'I said — is your name Ginger?' Taggart repeated.

Ginger glanced over his shoulder nervously, thinking about running. Jardine and Jackie Reid were already moving rapidly up the steps behind him, Jardine brandishing his ID card.

Ginger's shoulders slumped resignedly. It looked like a vice bust of some kind — although he thought that the police only ever arrested kerb crawlers. Whatever it was, co-operation seemed the most sensible course of action. He looked at Taggart again. 'Okay, so my name's Ginger. What's all this about?'

'Did you arrange to meet a girl called Jenny last night?' Jardine asked him.

There seemed no point in denying it. Ginger nodded. 'Yes, I arranged to meet her, but she didn't show up.'

'We're arresting you on suspicion of murder,' Taggart told

him flatly. 'You don't have to say anything, but anything you do say may be used in evidence.' Having made the statutory declaration, Taggart nodded to Jardine. 'All right, take him to the car, Michael.'

Ginger offered no resistance as Jardine gripped his arm firmly, turned him round and urged him to walk back down the steps towards the waiting car. He allowed himself to be bundled inside, saying nothing. In fact, he said nothing more at all until they were all installed in an interview room at Maryhill Police Station and he had started to recover somewhat from the shock of his arrest.

He regarded Taggart with a nervous, shifty look in his eyes. 'Look, I have a family. If I don't go home soon, I'm in trouble.'

'Oh, you're in trouble already, Ginger,' Taggart told him. 'Big trouble. Now, what time did you meet this girl, Jenny?'

'I told you, I never met her. I was supposed to, but she never turned up. I waited for about twenty minutes and then I left.'

'You just waited?' Jardine repeated.

Ginger nodded. 'That's right.'

'It didn't occur to you to phone her and find out where she was, what had happened to her?'

The man shook his head slowly. 'No.'

'Why not?' Taggart demanded. 'You had her number.'

'I just don't know. There didn't seem much point.'

'There was a phone-box about fifty yards away, just around the corner. You could have gone to that and phoned her,' Jardine pointed out.

'But I didn't. I told you, I just waited and then I left. It was getting late, I had to get home.' Ginger broke off and looked at his watch nervously.

'Is there a good reason why you didn't want to put yourself anywhere near that phone-box last night?' Taggart wanted to know.

Ginger was becoming increasingly edgy under the questioning. 'Look, how many times do I have to tell you? I didn't meet her, I didn't phone her. I just left.' He broke off, looking across at Taggart with a plea for male understanding in his eyes. 'You've got to understand — if I get home late, my wife asks questions, know what I mean?'

Taggart nodded, his face impassive. 'Oh, I know what you mean, Ginger. Guess you're in for a rough night then, aren't you?'

Ginger was silent for a while, contemplating his position. 'I never met her,' he repeated after a while.

'Well, someone did,' Taggart said firmly. 'She went to that phone-box to call us, and somebody stopped her.'

'Gingerbread,' Jardine said suddenly, watching the man's face closely for a reaction. 'Does that mean anything to you?'

There was only an expression of puzzlement. 'What?'

'Gingerbread,' Jardine repeated. 'It isn't a nickname your friends use?'

The man shook his head. 'They call me Ginger. That's bad enough.' He looked at Taggart again. 'Look, can I do a deal with you?'

'We don't do deals,' Taggart told him bluntly.

'I'll answer all the questions you want,' Ginger went on, trying nevertheless. 'Just let me go home to my family tonight so my wife doesn't ask questions — and I'll come back here in the morning.'

Taggart dashed his hopes once and for all. 'Sorry, Ginger. That's just the way it goes sometimes.' He nodded over to the uniformed officer standing by the door. 'Bang him up. Standard cover — "assisting the police with their enquiries".'

Taggart glanced across at Jardine as Ginger was led away to the cells. They exchanged a look of frustration. Both grim-faced, they returned to the main office.

'I take it he's not our man, sir?' Jackie said as they walked in.

Taggart glared at her. She sounded too positive, too damned sure of herself. 'We haven't finished with him yet,' he muttered defensively.

'But a guilty man would have denied knowing the girl,'

Jackie pointed out, stressing her case. 'He admitted going to meet her straight away.'

She was merely reinforcing Taggart's own instinctive opinion — but he didn't take kindly to having it spelled out by a junior officer. 'If you're so smart — *you* go and question him,' he said grumpily.

Jackie Reid got the message. Throwing an expressive look with her eyes at Jardine, she made a discreet and tactical withdrawal to the sidelines.

McVitie came out of his office and strode over towards them. 'Did you get anything out of Ginger?' he enquired optimistically.

Taggart regarded him glumly. 'Only that his real name is Ernest McGarrity and he likes a bit on the side, sir. Other than that, I think he's as bewildered as we are.'

McVitie nodded thoughtfully. 'I assume you're holding him?'

Taggart confirmed with a faint nod. 'We'll keep him till the morning and then question him again — but I really don't think we're going to learn very much more. Basically, I think we're at another dead end.'

It was not what McVitie wanted to hear. 'Anything from Dr Andrews on the rest of the body parts we unearthed in Jobson's back garden?'

'They didn't all belong to Phillip Chalmers, sir,' Jardine put in. 'There's another unidentified male.'

Taggart shot his colleague a withering look. 'You didn't tell me that,' he said testily.

Jardine looked apologetic. 'Sorry sir. The report was on my desk this morning. I forgot to pass it on.'

Taggart smiled understandingly, suddenly remembering why Jardine's concentration wasn't quite one hundred per cent. 'Why don't you go home?' he suggested. 'Haven't you got something to do?'

Jardine flushed slightly.

'Yes, you get on home, Mike,' Jackie added. 'I'll type up Ginger's interrogation report.'

Jardine took the hint. 'Right, I'll be off, then. See you in the morning.'

'Oh — and good luck,' Taggart called after him as he departed.

McVitie regarded him quizzically. 'Is there something I don't know?' he asked, slightly puzzled.

Chapter Twenty-five

Gemma was busy pounding away at the keyboard of her word processor as Jardine let himself into the flat. She looked up briefly at the sound of the door closing. 'Hi.'

Jardine walked over and bent down to kiss her. Gemma frowned slightly, pulling away from him. 'Can I just finish this sentence, Mike? It's the end of a chapter.'

Jardine got the message. He backed away as Gemma typed out another few words and pressed the 'save' key. She pushed herself away from the table and looked up at him with a little smile of satisfaction on her face.

Jardine made the most of his opportunity. Stepping forward again, he kissed her on the lips.

'So, how's it going?'

'Great,' Gemma said, beaming with enthusiasm. 'I've just finished the Black Pudding Shop murder. I've entitled it "Choice Cuts from the Meat Man". If you'd like to read it, I'll run a print-out for you.'

'Maybe later,' Jardine muttered. He crossed to the stereo

unit and selected some suitable mood music, slipping it on to the turntable.

'I'm going to start working on the Balfour kidnap case now,' Gemma carried on. 'I got a letter from Michael Balfour in Peterhead Prison, and he says that he's willing to meet me and tell me his side of it. Should be fascinating, don't you think?'

Gemma broke off, eyeing Jardine curiously as romantic music swelled from the loudspeakers and he turned back towards her, a purposeful look on his face.

Jardine walked across to the table, took her hands in his and gently lifted her to her feet. He led her across to the settee and urged her to sit down. 'I've got something I want to ask you,' he said quietly, sitting down beside her. He fished awkwardly in his pocket for the jewellery box.

'I bought this for you,' he said simply, handing it to her.

Gemma's eyes glittered with delight. 'Oh, Michael, you are sweet.' She flipped open the lid of the box and her face fell.

Jardine didn't notice. He was feeling awkward and embarrassed to look her directly in the eyes. 'It's an engagement ring,' he mumbled, rather superfluously. 'I bought it rather on impulse, so if it doesn't fit I'll have to take it back to the shop and have it altered.' He paused for a moment, giving a nervous little laugh. 'It's a bit better than the one I bought you sixteen years ago.'

Jardine looked up at her for the first time, to gauge her reaction. It was not what he had been expecting. Gemma stared at the ring, a slightly shocked look on her face.

'Oh, Mike,' she breathed. There was sadness in her voice.

Jardine's lower lip trembled nervously. 'Of course — if you want to think about it for a while. I know I should have asked you first.'

Gemma sighed deeply. She snapped the ring box shut and placed it on the arm of the settee. Turning back to Jardine, she grasped both of his hands. 'Mike, there's something I have to tell you,' she said in a very quiet and serious voice.

Jardine felt a sick, fluttering feeling in his belly. Something was horribly, terribly wrong. He chewed at his bottom lip. 'What is it?'

It was Gemma's turn to look nervous and embarrassed. 'I don't know how to say it,' she murmured.

Jardine squeezed her hands. 'Try,' he urged.

Gemma took a deep breath, not relishing what she had to say. It was going to hurt him deeply, she knew, but there could be no easy way of telling him. 'The truth is, Mike, I'm engaged already,' she said finally. 'His name's Derek, he's a journalist in London. I've known him for about three years.'

Gemma paused to let the shock of her news sink in. Jardine's face registered a kaleidoscope of emotions, running through shock, pain, disbelief and finally settling on anger.

'I was going to tell you,' Gemma went on. 'I just didn't think that you would do something like this.'

'Something like what? Fall in love with you all over again?' Jardine demanded bitterly. 'You moved in here with me, we slept together.'

'It was only temporary,' Gemma reminded him. 'We agreed that.'

Jardine jumped to his feet and paced angrily around the room for a few moments. Finally he stopped, whirling round to face her again.

'How can you be engaged? I don't understand.'

'Derek and I agreed on a testing period — a trial separation for three months in which we wouldn't see one another. We'd be free to see other people, live our own lives, work out if we really wanted to commit ourselves to each other.'

'And?' Jardine asked.

Gemma looked down at the floor. 'I love him, Mike,' she said simply.

'And me? What about me?'

She looked up at him, genuine fondness on her face. 'I think a lot of you, Mike. You're an old friend — a good friend. We go back a long way. I was going to tell you, eventually. I thought you'd understand.

Jardine regarded her with incomprehension. 'You thought

183

I'd *understand*? That you were sleeping with me just to convince yourself it was someone else you wanted to marry?'

Gemma shook her head distractedly. It wasn't going right, she wasn't explaining herself as she had meant to. She was still hurting him, even though she didn't want to. 'Oh, Mike, it wasn't like that. Or it wasn't meant to be.'

'Then what was it like?' Jardine demanded. 'You made all the running, right from the start. You flirted with me, led me along, gave me the idea that we could just pick things up where we left off. You *used* me, Gemma. You used me just to help you get your bloody stories.'

'No!' The denial was emphatic. 'Not that, Mike. I'm really fond of you. I didn't ever mean for you to get hurt. It was just a fling, like we had in the old days.'

It was those last words which finally got through to Jardine, made him understand at last. He was silent for a long while, finally sighing. When he spoke again, it was with a cold, resigned anger.

'That's all I ever was to you. Just a fling,' he observed. 'God, how could I have been so stupid.'

Gemma was almost crying now. 'You weren't stupid, Mike. I was,' she told him. 'When you grow up, everything becomes so much more complicated.'

Jardine sank down into an armchair, sighing heavily. He stared across the room towards the wall, seeing nothing. 'Just get your stuff together and get out,' he muttered thickly. 'Just go, go away and leave me alone.'

Gemma opened her mouth to argue, tell him that there was no need for them to part so bitterly, but no words came out. With a heavy heart, she stood up, crossed to the table and began to pick up the pages of her manuscript, tucking them into a folder. Silently she closed and locked her portable processor and picked it up by its carrying handle. She walked slowly towards the door.

'I'll pick the rest of my stuff up tomorrow, when you're at work,' she murmured quietly.

Then she was gone, closing the door quietly but firmly

behind her. Jardine buried his face in his hands and began to sob like a child. He cried for a long time.

The light of the twelve-volt inspection lamp cast an eerie glow through the darkened forest. In a small clearing, just off the access lane, Joe Soutar worked under the uplifted bonnet of his van, cursing himself for his impetuousness in starting to tinker with the engine so late in the evening.

It wasn't as if he was even a half-decent mechanic, he reminded himself bitterly. Other than knowing the engine basics, he was just fiddling in the dark, in more ways than one. And now he was stuck with the job, at least until he could put all the bits he had disconnected back together again. Wearily, he locked the distributor cap back in place and started to reconnect the HT leads.

Car headlights carved a path through the darkness. Soutar looked up, surprised to see a car coming up the lane towards Betty Duncan's cottage. A strange hour to come visiting, he thought, as the car continued all the way up to the front of the cottage and stopped. In the dim light from the cottage window, Soutar could just make out the figure of a man stepping out of the car and walking up to the front door. The door opened and the man walked in. Moments later a light went on in one of the upstairs rooms.

Soutar returned to his work, screwing the spark plugs back into place and reconnecting them. Just a few more things to check and he'd be ready to try and start the van. With a bit of luck, he would be able to limp it home and get it to a proper garage in the morning, as he should have done in the first place.

A blood-curdling scream sliced through the silence of the night, echoing between the trees. The sudden shock made Soutar jump, his head connecting painfully with the raised bonnet. Slightly dazed, he stepped back from the van and stared towards the cottage. The scream had to have come from there. Thinking of Betty, Soutar shook the pain in his head away and began to run towards the house.

The back door was unlocked. Soutar threw it open, dashing into the kitchen. It was empty. His eyes fell upon the gingerbread house which still sat, untouched, upon the kitchen table.

Even as he looked at it, a red stain suddenly blossomed out upon the virgin white icing of the roof. It was quickly followed by another, and another.

With a sense of foreboding, Soutar's eyes travelled upwards to the ceiling, where a red, sticky patch had begun to spread out around the rose of the light fitting, forming into thick liquid droplets. Two more blobs detached themselves from the ceiling and fell upon the roof of the gingerbread house, splashing into a star-like pattern. Soutar's stomach turned to jelly as the drops of blood turned to a thin trickle, pouring over the gingerbread house and spattering on to the tiny figurines of Hansel, Gretel and the witch.

The queasiness in his stomach settled down suddenly, hardening into a cold, tight knot of horror. Adrenaline flooded into Soutar's system, washing away caution and fear. Thinking only of Betty's safety, Soutar ran to the foot of the stairs and charged up them towards the landing.

The door at the top of the stairs was slightly ajar. Soutar moved more cautiously now, pushing it with his fingertips. 'Betty?' he called quietly as the door began to swing open. There was no answer. Soutar peered into the room as the door opened fully.

His stomach churned. Bile and vomit rose in his throat, making him gag. The grisly sight which greeted his eyes, and the sickly stench of blood which assaulted his nostrils, was enough to make the strongest man go weak at the knees.

Soutar froze rigid, his heart pounding in his chest. Transfixed with horror and revulsion, there was nothing he could do except let his eyes and brain try to take in the full extent of the carnage inside the room.

It was to be the last thing he ever saw. Behind him, Betty Duncan stepped silently into position, her legs braced slightly apart and an axe held high in the air above her head.

Soutar heard only a faint grunt of exertion before the wicked blade cleaved downwards, biting deep into his skull.

The doorbell rang. Jardine looked up with red-rimmed eyes, his face a taut mask of misery. He made no move to get up to answer it. The bell rang again, this time longer and more insistently.

Reluctantly, he pushed himself to his feet and moved slowly towards the door. He opened it, fully expecting to see Gemma standing there.

Instead, it was Simon. Without waiting for an invitation, the boy pushed himself past Jardine and walked into the living-room. Jardine sighed deeply.

'This is the wrong time, Simon,' he muttered heavily.

Simon stood in the middle of the room, adopting an aggressive stance. 'I'm not going back there,' he announced.

'You have to, Simon,' Jardine told him firmly. 'I'm going to call the Frazers right now and tell them I'm bringing you back immediately.' He moved towards the telephone.

'Please, Mike.' Simon ran after him, clutching at his arm. The sad, almost desperate expression on his face reinforced the plea in his eyes.

Jardine relented, sensing how deeply disturbed the boy was. Thinking about what Simon had been through in the last few weeks seemed to make his own problems almost trivial by comparison.

'All right, you can stay here tonight — but I'm taking you back first thing in the morning,' Jardine told him. 'I'll just phone Mr and Mrs Frazer and tell them you're safe.'

Simon nodded, accepting the compromise. He moved over to the settee and sat down as Jardine went to make the phone call.

Later, over two cups of steaming cocoa, he eyed Jardine concernedly. 'Why was tonight the wrong time?' he asked.

Jardine tried to shrug off the question. 'It's just been a

long hard day,' he lied.

Simon wasn't to be fooled. 'I saw Gemma downstairs earlier,' he said. 'She'd been crying, too.'

Despite himself, Jardine found himself giving the boy a thin smile. 'Some day, Simon, your powers of detection are going to land you in deep trouble.'

'Have you split up?' Simon wanted to know.

'Jardine nodded. 'Yes.'

'I'm sorry,' Simon said, with genuine concern. 'She was nice.'

'Yes, she was,' Jardine agreed, and fell silent.

Simon regarded him very seriously. 'You'll get over it, won't you?' he asked, a strange little catch to his voice. 'I mean, people do get over most things, don't they?'

Jardine looked at him with a sudden wave of sympathy and understanding. They both knew Simon was referring to himself. 'Yes, Simon,' Jardine assured the boy. 'People get over most things, given time.'

Simon was quiet for a long while, thinking deeply. When he spoke again, there was a definite mistiness to his eyes. 'I miss him,' he said simply.

Jardine slipped his arm around the boy's shoulders in a paternal gesture. 'I know you do, Simon. And I know that you've been trying to cope with it in the best way you can.'

'It's just that I wonder about a lot of things,' Simon went on. 'Like I wonder if I could have saved him that night — if I hadn't run away.'

As simply as that, it was all out in the open, everything was clear. Jardine understood, suddenly, what had been driving the boy for the past weeks, the secret fear which had been tormenting him.

It was time to set the record straight, Jardine thought. He looked Simon directly in the eyes, speaking in a firm, authoritative tone. 'You didn't run away, Simon. You got your little sister out of the house — to safety. That was quick thinking.' Jardine paused for a moment, considering his next words carefully. 'And there was nothing you could have done to save your father's life, you must believe that. There was nothing anyone could have done.'

Simon nodded thoughtfully, taking it in. 'I just wondered,' he said quietly.

Jardine shook his head slowly. 'No, Simon. You've been doing a lot more than just wondering. I think it's been on your mind a lot.'

The boy's eyes were looking heavy and tired. Jardine consulted his watch, surprised to find it was well after eleven o'clock. He took the almost empty mug of cocoa from Simon's hand and set it down on the coffee-table.

'Come on, Simon. I guess we'll both feel better for a good night's sleep,' he suggested.

Chapter Twenty-six

Jardine put two plates of bacon and scrambled eggs down on the breakfast table and went back to the kitchen to make a pot of tea. When he returned Simon was already tucking in as though he had been starved for a week.

'Can I come in to the police station with you today?' Simon asked, speaking with his mouth full.

'No chance,' Jardine told him flatly. 'The first thing you're going to do today is go back to Mrs Duncan and apologise to her for breaking into her house.'

Simon froze, a forkful of scrambled egg halfway to his mouth. There was a look of alarm in his eyes. 'I can't go back there. I told you, she's mad.'

Jardine dismissed the objection. 'You can't betray someone's trust by sneaking in when they're not there and snooping around. We have to get search warrants for that, you know.'

Simon racked his brain for another excuse. 'There's something else. She's got somebody living upstairs. In a locked room.'

Jardine looked at the boy with exasperation. 'Are you sure it's not something locked away in the cellar?' he asked with a trace of sarcasm.

'Look, Simon — millions of people have lodgers, or friends staying in their houses. Why do you have to insist that there's something sinister about an old lady living in a cottage in the woods?'

Simon was defiant. 'She's not just an old lady,' he maintained.

Jardine laid down his knife and fork with a sigh. 'Just give me one single reason why she should have anything to do with your father's death.'

Simon thought for a while. 'Dad took us there the day before he died.'

Jardine smiled indulgently at the boy. 'And that's your evidence, is it? Your father took you blackberry-picking in the woods, so the old lady living in the cottage must be a murderer.' Jardine broke off, shaking his head ruefully. 'Come on, Simon — you'll have to do better than that.'

Jardine was tired of the silly excuses. He'd had enough. 'Now look, Simon — I'll tell you what we're going to do. I'll phone Mrs Duncan first and prepare the ground for you. How about that?'

Simon saw the fixed, purposeful expression on Jardine's face and realised that he had come to the end of the line. With great reluctance he fished in his pocket and drew out a slip of paper with Betty Duncan's telephone number written on it. Wordlessly, he handed it to Jardine, who scanned it quickly before slipping it into his pocket.

The doorbell rang. 'That'll be Mr Brockwell,' Jardine announced, getting up. 'He said he'd come round and pick you up.'

Simon glared after him as Jardine went to answer the door, feeling a sense of betrayal. He greeted Brockwell with a distinct lack of enthusiasm as Jardine showed him into the breakfast room.

'Well, I'd better get ready to go on duty,' Jardine muttered, sensing the tense atmosphere. He made a discreet exit.

Brockwell sat down at the table opposite Simon and stared at him for some time. 'Well, young man,' he said finally. 'We're going to have to find some way of stopping these little escapades of yours, aren't we?'

The words were apparently harmless enough, and Brockwell had a smile on his face as he spoke, but Simon imagined that he detected a distinct sense of threat.

Betty Duncan raked the earth under the base of the still-smouldering incinerator. Pausing in her efforts, she looked across towards the lane where Soutar's van and trailer still stood. Betty's haggard face creased into a frown. It was a problem which she had yet to contend with.

She sighed heavily, wearily. As if she didn't have enough to worry about already, she reflected miserably. Her face grim, she dropped the rake and picked up the half-full can of petrol, carrying it towards the cottage. There was a terrible tiredness, almost desperation, in her step.

She laid the petrol can down just inside the back door. Suddenly seeming very weak and frail, she shuffled across to a stool by the Aga cooker and flopped down. Her eyes strayed to the kitchen table, and the bloodstained gingerbread house. Behind her, on the stove, a kettle of water began to boil, but she ignored it.

Finally tearing her eyes away from the gory confection on the table, she turned and stared blankly out through the kitchen window towards the forest.

She sat there, rock-still, for a long time, her aged face appearing to carry all the sadness and suffering of the world. Wearily she pushed herself to her feet. There were still unpleasant chores to do. She crossed to the sink, ran the hot tap and began to scrub the bloodstained axe which was lying on it.

Music swelled out suddenly from upstairs. Betty paused in her work, her eyes straying fearfully up to the ceiling before returning to the job in hand.

Incongruously, she continued to scrub the caked and dried blood from the blade of the axe as the strains of 'Carolina Moon' filled the cottage.

Simon stared out of the window of Brockwell's van with a growing sense of unease. He turned to the man beside him. 'This isn't the way back to the house,' he pointed out. 'Where are we going?'

Brockwell smiled thinly. 'To see Mrs Duncan,' he announced.

Fear showed on Simon's face. 'I don't want to go back there,' he said urgently.

'You have to.' Brockwell was adamant. 'Sergeant Jardine said you should go and apologise for breaking into her cottage.'

'I didn't break in,' Simon protested. 'The door was open. I just walked in to take a look around. I didn't mean any harm.'

Brockwell's face was unforgiving. 'You were in the wrong.' he said sternly. 'And now you have to face the consequences.' He concentrated on the road ahead, ignoring Simon's anguished face.

'But she's mad,' the boy blurted out, rising panic in his voice.

The argument had no effect on Brockwell. 'Nonsense,' he snapped. 'She's probably just a little eccentric, that's all. Elderly people become a trifle eccentric sometimes.'

It was no use, Simon thought bitterly. No one took the slightest notice of anything he said. Nobody believed him. The entire world of grown-ups had somehow conspired against him. Sullen-faced, he lapsed into silence.

There was a small reception committee waiting for Jardine as he walked into the main office. A ragged chorus of 'For He's a Jolly Good Fellow' started up. Someone threw a handful of confetti over his head as he walked past. There were various banners and notices pinned up on the walls, along with a couple of condoms blown up like balloons. Even Taggart stood in the doorway of his office, an uncharacteristic smile of welcome on his face.

Under other circumstances Jardine would have appreciated the gesture. This morning, however, it was about as welcome as a jar of treacle would be to a diabetic. Looking distinctly unamused, Jardine marched straight across the office to his desk and sat down. He took the piece of paper with Betty Duncan's number on it out of his pocket, picked up the phone and started to dial.

The song faded into an awkward and embarrassed silence. Jackie Reid stepped over to Jardine's side.

'Well?'

Jardine glared up at her. 'Well what?'

'Are congratulations in order?'

Jardine's grim expression gave her the answer.

'Turn you down, did she?' Taggart asked, rather tactlessly.

Jardine cast a withering look in his direction. '*I* turned *her* down,' he muttered. 'I threw her out of my flat.'

He finished dialling the number, to be greeted by the engaged tone. Fuming with frustration, Jardine slammed the receiver back into the cradle. He stood up, addressing the entire office. 'Just to stop all sorts of wild stories going round, I'll tell you all the facts once and for all. She already had a fiancé she'd neglected to tell me about.'

He sat down again. Jackie fussed round him sympathetically. 'Oh, Mike, I'm sorry.'

Jardine grunted. 'Yeah, so am I.'

McVitie walked into the office, accompanied by Gault. Once again there was a slightly bemused expression on his face as he sensed the strained atmosphere in the room but couldn't put his finger on the cause. The two men headed straight for Taggart's office.

Taggart ushered them in, nodding over to Jardine and Jackie to request their presence. Jardine followed Jackie into the office, closing the door behind him.

'I found three prostitutes in Edinburgh who had dealings with Phillip Chalmers,' Gault announced when they were all assembled. 'Two of them work in a massage parlour in Cockburn Street, the third was altogether more interesting. A Miss Rebecca Wilson. Part-time city tour guide, part-time escort girl.'

'Sounds like quite a tour,' Taggart put in with a wry grin.

'It seems she got into the business as a kind of dare,' Gault went on. 'She met Chalmers through an agency and they became quite close. He used to take her away for weekends, to special functions — that sort of thing.'

'Risky profession to take up as a dare,' McVitie put in.

Gault looked at him, a slightly superior smile on his face. 'Perhaps I should explain that we're talking special services here,' he pointed out. 'It seems that Phillip Chalmers had quite specific sexual preferences. What one might call fantasy wish-fulfilment, for want of a better term.'

'Well, he certainly got a special service here in Glasgow,' Taggart observed with black humour.

Gault was not amused. 'The point being,' he stressed, in case they had all missed it, 'we are probably not looking for some ordinary two-bit tart. As I said, Phillip's peculiar and personal tastes required a highly individual service.'

'So it's possible that he only went to one person here in Glasgow,' Taggart observed, taking Gault's point.

Gault nodded. 'Right. And that person may well have been directly, or indirectly, responsible for his death.'

'But that still doesn't put us any closer to finding out where, or why,' McVitie said. 'Or, indeed, how this connects up with the murder of Tom Barrow.'

'Then that's what we have to find out, sir,' Taggart said.

Jackie Reid nudged Jardine gently in the ribs. 'I think that's the cue for us to get back to work.' She stood up, addressing the company in general. 'So, what are we actually looking for? A crazy female with a razor or a jealous boy-friend with one?'

Gault started to light up a yellow cigarette, much to Taggart's annoyance. 'Perhaps we should look for both,' he suggested.

Chapter Twenty-seven

'So now you know everything,' Jardine said to Jackie as she drove them into the heart of the red light district again.

He had told her the full story of his relationship with Gemma, not so much because she had asked but because she specifically had *not* asked. Oddly enough, it felt better to get it off his chest, share it with someone else. And he trusted Jackie Reid as a confidante. She might have a nasty edge to her tongue at times, but it was never loose. Jardine felt secure in the belief that she would never betray a confidence.

'One more thing,' he added as a codicil. 'Just don't say you told me so.'

Jackie shrugged faintly. 'Well, let's just say that I did try to warn you, Mike. But then I didn't really expect you to listen. I probably wouldn't have if things had been the other way round.' She paused thoughtfully. 'And I'll say one thing more now, as a friend. Forget her. She's not worth worrying about.'

Jardine smiled ruefully. 'Easier said than done,' he murmured.

'Actually, I think you're being remarkably calm and adult about the whole thing,' Jackie went on. 'If a guy did that to me, I think I'd kill him.'

Jardine shook his head. 'No, you wouldn't,' he assured her. 'Something would hold you back — like it held me back last night.'

She was far from convinced on this point. 'But for someone to be that callous, that deceitful . . .' She didn't finish the sentence.

Jardine smiled wistfully. 'Oh, she wasn't always like that,' he murmured, remembering better times. He looked ahead through the windscreen, seeing a phone-box on the corner of the next intersection. 'Look, do you mind pulling in by that phone-box?'

Jackie glanced at him with concern. 'Mike, you're not still hoping she'll change her mind?'

Jardine shook his head firmly. 'No. I just want to close it while I'm thinking rationally. Which I wasn't last night.'

Jackie pulled the car to a halt beside the phone-box. Jardine started to climb out. 'I won't be long. I just want to catch her while she's still at her mother's house. Just a few well-chosen words, that's all.'

He walked into the phone-box, took out his address book and started to tap out the number. As he waited for an answer, his eyes fell upon a small white visiting card tucked into the side of the coin box.

His call was answered. 'Hello, Mrs Normanton? It's Mike Jardine. Could I speak to Gemma, please?'

As he spoke Jardine's finger strayed to the card, picking it up.

'You mean she didn't come home last night?' he said in surprise, as Gemma's mother answered him.

He turned the white card over, reading the message printed on it.

'GINGERBREAD GIRLS'
ESCORT SERVICE
Make Your Fantasies
Come True

198

The message was followed by a Glasgow telephone number.

Jardine's entire system jolted into hyperdrive. 'Look, I'm sorry, Mrs Normanton — but I have to go,' he blurted into the phone, slamming it back into its cradle. He pushed open the door of the phone-box, sprinting towards the car and jumping in.

'Get back to base — fast,' he barked at Jackie.

Taggart tapped the card against his fingers. 'This must be what Jenny was trying to tell us. Not Gingerbread Men, but Gingerbread *Girls*.'

'And it all makes sense now, it ties up,' Jackie added. 'The guilty phone calls home. Telling their wives they loved them, making excuses.'

Taggart handed the card back to Jardine. 'Make a call, Mike. Pretend you're a punter.'

Jardine took the card, a slight frown on his face. 'Suppose she asks what sort of thing I'm into?' he queried.

'Just don't say the missionary position,' Jackie suggested, grinning. The ill-timed attempt at humour earned her a baleful glare from Taggart, who was not amused.

Jardine sat down at his desk and reached for the phone. Studying the number on the card, he began to punch out the digits. Halfway through he paused, dropping the phone back in its rest. There was something oddly familiar about the number, he realised. The first flutterings of alarm had started deep in his belly.

'What is it?' Taggart wanted to know at once, sensing something was wrong.

Jardine was fishing frantically in his pocket, becoming increasingly agitated. Eventually he pulled out the scrap of paper which Simon had given him and laid it out on his desktop. As he checked Betty Duncan's phone number, his worst fears were confirmed.

Jardine's face had gone ashen. His hands were trembling.

The full horror of the situation had only just begun to sink in.

'Mike — what the hell is it?' Taggart demanded again.

Jardine's voice was shaky. He had to force the words out. 'It's the same number. Gingerbread Girls and Betty Duncan's cottage.'

He broke off, looking up at Taggart in fear. 'And I've just sent Simon back there!'

Brockwell pulled to a halt beside Soutar's abandoned van and trailer. He turned to Simon. 'Right then, Simon. Off you go to apologise to Mrs Duncan, and I'll see you later.'

Alarm showed on the boy's face. 'Aren't you coming in with me?'

'No, I am not,' Brockwell said firmly. 'I have a children's party in half an hour. Balloon magic and ventriloquism. Besides, you don't need me.'

Brockwell got out of the van and opened the rear doors, pulling out Simon's bike and resting it against Soutar's trailer. He looked at Simon again with a stern expression on his face. 'We all have to grow up and fight our own battles, young man.'

Simon regarded the man miserably. He didn't want to fight a battle. He didn't even want to grow up if it meant turning the sort of adult he had observed recently. Adults hurt each other, let each other down, refused to believe the truth even when it was thrust under their noses. But most of all, Simon didn't want to go back into that cottage, to face a mad old woman who might have killed his father.

Brockwell was already climbing back into the van, preparing to turn round and drive away. Reluctantly, Simon picked up his bike and began to push it towards the cottage, feeling a sense of total abandonment.

Betty Duncan's black cat sat in the yard, crouching like some mythical sentinel from the netherworld. It hissed warningly at Simon as he approached, its eyes flashing fire.

The breeze wafted a thin mist of smoke in Simon's direction from the still-smouldering incinerator. He wrinkled his nose in disgust at the particularly acrid smell, shuddering instinctively even though he had no memory or knowledge to tell him it was the stench of charred flesh.

The cat spat out a last gesture of defiance and slunk away. Simon lowered his bike to the ground and walked the last few yards to the back door. He stopped, turning round as the grating sound of Brockwell's starter motor suddenly broke the silence. The man had managed to stall the van whilst trying to turn in the narrow lane, and was now trying to get the battered vehicle going again.

For a moment Simon seriously considered the possibility of running back to Brockwell, pleading with him to take him away. But he probably wouldn't listen, Simon realised with a sinking heart. Nobody listened to him.

With a last hopeless look in the direction of the van, Simon turned back to the door. It was slightly ajar. He pushed it with his fingertips, peering into the cottage kitchen as it swung fully open.

'Mrs Duncan!' he called out.

There was no answer. Warily Simon stepped into the kitchen and looked around. His eyes fell on the bloodstained gingerbread house on the table. Driven by a sense of morbid curiosity, Simon stepped towards it, nearly knocking over a bucket of water and a mop which was sitting in the middle of the kitchen floor.

He gazed at the gingerbread house for a long time, finally allowing his eyes to wander up to the ceiling with its dark red stain.

'Mrs Duncan !' he called again, a little louder.

Again there was no response, but the light fitting quivered slightly and there was the unmistakable sound of hurried footsteps from upstairs.

Simon moved slowly towards the stairs. Gripping the banister rail tightly, he began to creep up towards the landing.

The door which had previously been locked was now slightly ajar. Simon froze, looking at it uncertainly. The footsteps had undoubtedly come from inside that room. His heart thumping, Simon forced himself to move forward, pushing the door open with his foot.

At first glance the room seemed empty and perfectly normal. There were the usual furnishings — a bed, a dressing-table, lamp and shelves with china ornaments upon them. A record player sat on the floor, its lid up and an empty album sleeve propped up against it.

Suddenly, Simon noticed the huge bloodstain on the carpet near the foot of the bed. He stepped into the room to examine it more closely.

The door slammed shut behind him. Simon whirled round, his mouth opening in a silent scream as the figure of Ann Kirk sprang out from where she had been hiding behind the door.

The woman's face was contorted into an evil mask of hate, her thin lips drawn back across clenched teeth. Her eyes flashed madly as she confronted him, poised like a dangerous animal about to pounce. With her black hair and glinting eyes, she reminded Simon of a large, black evil cat.

But this cat did not just have sharp talons. This cat wielded the gleaming, flesh-slicing blade of an open razor.

All the horror of his father's murder flooded back into Simon's mind, lending him strength, speed and the will to fight. He practically jumped across the room to the open window, screaming at the top of his voice to Brockwell.

He was only a second or so too late. The van coughed into life at last, and began to bump away down the lane.

Ann Kirk's hand clamped over his mouth from behind, pulling his head back to expose his throat. Death was only a moment away, Simon realised, and this certain, terrible knowledge was enough to give him one last and desperate burst of energy.

He lashed backwards with his foot, at the same time clamping his teeth tightly into the fleshy part of the hand over his mouth. Ann screamed with the sudden and unexpected pain in her hand and shin, reeling back with the shock. Simon bolted for the door, wrenching it open and bounding down the stairs towards the open back door and freedom.

Betty Duncan stepped into the doorway from outside the cottage, blocking his escape. Trapped, Simon could only cast his eyes desperately around for another way out as Ann ran down the stairs behind him.

There was none. All hope gone, and with the last ounce of fight knocked out of him, Simon froze with indecision like a trapped rabbit.

Ann Kirk gripped his shoulders firmly, pushing him across the kitchen towards the barred door of the game larder. Throwing it open, she bundled him roughly inside and threw the bolt across on the outside, imprisoning him like an animal in a cage.

'Let him out of there, Ann. Let the boy go.' Betty Duncan's voice was firm and authoritative.

Ann Kirk whirled on her, spitting hate and defiance. 'Mum, he's seen too much. He knows everything. It's all your bloody fault. If you hadn't encouraged him here in the first place . . .'

Betty sighed wearily. 'Things have gone too far now, Ann. It's over, it's all over.'

'No!' Ann screamed out the denial. 'They're not going to put me away again. Never again. Never again.'

Betty stepped into the cottage, moving towards her daughter. There was a desperately sad, pitying look on her face. 'It's the only thing, Ann,' she said gently, almost reassuringly. 'The killing has to stop, now. I should have had the strength to stop it myself years ago, but I was too weak.'

Ann threw her hands over her ears to shut out the words, shaking her head wildly from side to side. Her eyes rolled madly in their sockets. From his prison Simon watched the woman through the barred door in shocked terror. It was obvious that she was totally and dangerously insane.

'I'll not let you hurt the boy,' Betty went on in a strangely calm voice.

Ann suddenly let out a little scream of mad laughter. 'That's right — protect him. Just like you protected us.'

'That's enough, Ann,' Betty said sharply.

'Oh, no, that's not enough.' Ann shook her head violently again. 'Why don't we tell him the whole truth? Tell Simon what you were. What you turned your children into? Why they took us away from you and locked us up in that horrible place?'

Betty's voice had a tremor in it as she spoke again. 'Don't Ann. Stop it, now.'

Ann pressed her head against the bars of the game larder. She pulled back her hair, showing her scarred face to Simon. 'You see this, Simon? This sweet old lady fixed me up with a client who did this to me. Just like she fixed me and my sister up with all the other men who wanted to hurt us, do filthy things to us. Well, now she's paying for it, along with all the rest of them.'

Betty slumped against the side of the kitchen table, her face anguished and drawn. 'Haven't you punished me enough, Ann? All these years, I've had to cover up your insane killings, dispose of the bodies for you. Now you've turned me into a killer too, murdering poor old Joe who never hurt a fly.'

Again that crazy half-laugh, half snort of disgust. 'Enough? Oh no, I've only just got started.' She stared at her mother with contempt in her eyes. 'We were just kids. What chance did we have?'

'We needed the money. To feed you, buy clothes,' Betty muttered.

It was this last sickening attempt at self-justification which seemed to snap the final thread of whatever filial bond the two women had ever shared. Ann regarded Betty with undisguised loathing. 'We were *children*, you evil old bitch,' she spat out.

Ann turned her attention back to Simon, cowering in the game larder. 'And you, you meddling little brat. Now you'll have to pay, too.'

She crossed to the Aga cooker, drawing out the poker which had been resting in the glowing coals. Holding it by its insulated handle, Ann brandished the glowing, red-hot end in

Simon's direction. 'Now you're going to tell me who was in that van which drove away. Who else have you told about this place?'

Simon shrank back in terror as the woman advanced on him.

Betty pushed herself away from the kitchen table where she had been leaning. She threw herself at her daughter, clutching desperately at her arm and trying to hold her back. 'I told you, you mustn't hurt the boy,' she screamed.

Ann lashed out at her with her arm, catching Betty across the side of the head. The old woman fell back, half-stunned, lost her footing and collapsed to the floor near the back door. Ignoring her, Ann continued to advance towards Simon, holding the glowing poker out in front of her.

'No!' Betty screamed out in protest from the floor. Not thinking clearly, she grabbed the nearest object to hand and flung it at her daughter with all her strength.

The half-full petrol can flew through the air, spewing fuel from its unclipped spout. It struck Ann heavily on the back of the head, dousing her with petrol and knocking the poker from her hand. The petrol can fell to the floor, the last half gallon or so of its contents quickly spreading into a widely flowing pool.

Almost in slow motion, the thin pool of liquid crept across the last few inches of the floor to where the poker lay, its end still glowing red-hot. Ann Kirk saw the danger too late, turning to run — but the fuel had ignited with a dull *whoosh* and the flames were eagerly licking across the floor towards her.

Ann let out a terrible, high-pitched scream of fear and horror as the flames reached her feet and shot up her body with a sudden and savage burst of acceleration. In a split second her body was a living pillar of fire. Screaming horribly, her arms flailing wildly, she spun and stumbled across the kitchen in a series of fiery pirouettes, finally crashing against the table and collapsing over the bloodstained gingerbread house.

After that there was no more movement, except for the slow collapse of the witch figure as it melted in the heat.

Sobbing, Betty threw herself across the kitchen to the game larder, where Simon stood totally paralysed with horror. Throwing back the bolt, she half-pushed, half-dragged him out and bundled him towards the back door.

Clear of the cottage, Betty let the boy fall to the ground and collapsed beside him. They both lay there silently, unmoving, as the faint sounds of a police-car siren in the distance drew nearer and nearer.

Chapter Twenty-eight

Jardine and Taggart stood silently watching the burning cottage as uniformed officers led Betty Duncan to the waiting police car and shut her inside.

Simon stood some distance away being comforted by Jackie Reid. He stared across at Jardine, a bitter accusatory look in his eyes. Finally he detached himself from Jackie and walked over. He looked up into Jardine's face.

'I was right, wasn't I?' he demanded. There was both bitterness and triumph in his voice.

Jardine could not quite bring himself to face the boy directly. He glanced away as he answered. 'Yes, you were right, Simon,' he murmured in a soft, vaguely apologetic voice.

Simon walked away without another word, climbing into another police car as the door was opened for him. The car drove away, slowly. Simon did not look back.

Taggart stared after the departing car for a few seconds. He turned back, glancing up at Jardine with a grim smile on his face. 'I think he takes the credit for this one, right enough.'

'I found the card, sir,' Jardine muttered, feeling a sense of slight.

'Long before that,' Taggart observed. 'You had all the information right from the start. From Simon. His father was reccying this place — that's why he brought them here.'

Now Jardine was really indignant. 'How were any of us supposed to know that?' he demanded.

But Taggart was unforgiving. 'You should have spent more time listening to him and less time chasing your love life.'

There was a pained look on Jardine's face. 'You really know how to make me feel good, don't you, sir?' he muttered bitterly. He stormed away towards the incinerator where a police team were about to start excavations.

'Don't you think you were a little bit hard on him, sir?' Jackie asked Taggart. She had approached them just in time to hear the tail end of the conversation.

She didn't wait for an answer. Walking away, she caught up with Jardine and slipped her arm around his waist, commiserating with him.

Taggart smiled thinly, relenting a little. He called after them. 'Oh, Michael. Life isn't always a fairy-tale, you know?'

He turned and began to walk towards his car, reflecting on the truth of that remark.

Sometimes there was no happy ending, and people didn't live happily ever after.